BLOOD STAINS OF A SHOTTA 3

Lock Down Publications and Ca$h
Presents
BLOOD STAINS OF A SHOTTA 3
A Novel by *Jamaica*

Blood Stains of a Shotta 3

Lock Down Publications
P.O. Box 870494
Mesquite, Tx 75187

Copyright 2020 by Jamaica
BLOOD STAINS OF A SHOTTA 3

All rights reserved. No part of this book may be reproduced in any form or by electronic or mechanical means, including information storage and retrieval systems without permission in writing from the publisher, except by a reviewer who may quote brief passages in review.
First Edition January 2020
Printed in the United States of America

This is a work of fiction. Names, characters, places, and incidents either are products of the author's imagination or are used fictitiously. Any similarity to actual events or locales or persons, living or dead, is entirely coincidental.

Lock Down Publications
Like our page on Facebook: Lock Down Publications @
www.facebook.com/lockdownpublications.ldp
Cover design and layout by: **Dynasty Cover Me**
Book interior design by: **Shawn Walker**
Edited by: **Lashonda Johnson**

Jamaica

Stay Connected with Us!

Text **LOCKDOWN** to 22828 to stay up-to-date with new releases, sneak peaks, contests and more…

Thank you!

Submission Guideline.

Submit the first three chapters of your completed manuscript to ldpsubmissions@gmail.com, subject line: Your book's title. The manuscript must be in a .doc file and sent as an attachment. Document should be in Times New Roman, double spaced and in size 12 font. Also, provide your synopsis and full contact information. If sending multiple submissions, they must each be in a separate email.

Have a story but no way to send it electronically? You can still submit to LDP/Ca$h Presents. Send in the first three chapters, written or typed, of your completed manuscript to:

LDP: Submissions Dept
Po Box 870494
Mesquite, Tx 75187

DO NOT send original manuscript. Must be a duplicate.

Provide your synopsis and a cover letter containing your full contact information.

Thanks for considering LDP and Ca$h Presents.

Jamaica

ACKNOWLEDGEMENTS

Lord thank you for blessing me with this gift of creativity. I never thought in a million years that I would be an author. 6 books and counting...Everything happens for a reason, yea they trapped my body, but they never got the chance to capture my mind. Thank you for your grace, love and mercy.

Oswald and Julia James, Mama and Papa, thank you for opening your doors, heart and soul to me and taking the responsibility to raise me after y'all had finished raising y'all own kids. I am so blessed to have grandparents like you two. Mama, your words will always dwell inside of me, your love and support means the world to me, thank you for never judging me and for always loving me, unconditionally. Papa, even though I am older, I will always be your "Sweet Pea". You motivate me to go harder, all those early lessons that you taught me, came in handy. They can't hold me back or down, I am a James Breed baby. I love y'all with everything that is in me. Jeezy~~~ The Real MVP...

Tameia, baby girl. I don't know what I would have done without you. Your strength as an eleven year old girl is mind blowing. You inspire me to be the greatest in everything that I do. Your realness scares me, but I am so happy that we have that bond, where you tell me everything. I love you with my soul, and thank you, thank you for always having my back. They can't say nothing about me. As you would say, "Stay real and true!" Kevin Gates~~~ Betta For You...

Tamaine Jr., son, I love you with all of my heart and soul. I want you to always know that, no matter what. I know you can't wait for me to get home and I can't wait to get there either. It's just US 3! Real talk. I know you are having a hard time, but stay strong, we are going to make it. I have so much faith in you! And thank you for always worrying about me, but you don't need to, mommie got this. Remember to always stare a person in their eyes when you talk to them and your word is all that YOU have and you have to stand on it, hands down. Boosie~~~Me and Mama...

Leather, mane oh mane, what a year 2019 was for you, but through it all, you held it down... I owe you so much, mane, you just don't even know. God blessed me with you, he knew I needed you in my life. You know my word is 1000, and you already know, I GOT YOU! Thanks for raising my babies for me. I love you, lady!

Ca$h, I don't even know what I would have done without you, your love and support is that. Mane, you're always there when I need you, real talk. My loyalty will always be with YOU. Thanks for pushing me with this book right here, I was in a very dark place, felt like I was drowning, but with your help and motivation, I got this joint done. I am so sorry for missing all my deadlines, mane. How much bread I owe you, again? LOL... I love you though, real talk. Jeezy~~~Let's Get It/The Sky is The Limit (You stay preaching that shit to me, I got!)

Boss aka THE UNICOR President, G. Walker. Where do I begin thugga, look at me right now, I should be back in lane 21 working, but I am not, cause that job don't go out until tomorrow, so fuck dat shit right now, but you know Imma get that shit done though, or do I have to show you again that I am a BEAST, I'm ya best expeditor... On some real shit though,

Jamaica

thank you for allowing me to have 2 damn jobs at the same damn time. My kids gotta eat off this shit and you respect that and I respect you for allowing me to do that. You are a real ass person and you don't let that badge get to ya head and you treat us like humans... NBA Young Boy~~~Lonely Child

To my FANS, mane, especially the ones that are caged up, thank you for always reaching out and showing me mad love. I can't write back right now, cause the BOP be on some fuck shit with the mail for 3way, but know this, as soon as I am FREE, y'all will be hearing from me. I've written down y'all information and I promise to show that same love back and more. To the STREET FANS/READERS, thank YOU. I know it took me forever getting this joint out, but I was and I'm still dealing with some problems, but I had to push all that shit to the back and get this to Y'ALL. Once again, without y'all, I wouldn't be who I am in this book game... Jeezy~~Streets On Lock

To my homies/friends, most of y'all are like FAMILY because LOYALTY created that. Thank you guys for having my back. #Team Jamaica is REAL. Ca$h is gonna be hella mad with me on the next joint cause I am going to be showing mad love to each and everyone that's been with me... Boosie~~~Real Friends

LDP, we are a TEAM, that's unstoppable... THE GAME IS OURS!!!

Jeezy and Boosie, thanks for always dropping them bangerz. NBA Young Boy, Kevin Gates, and Yo Gotti, I can't even lie, I'm a FAN!!!

Blood Stains of a Shotta 3

Free all the real ones, stay strong, stay real, duck the haters, stay grounded, but most of all stay PRAYED UP!!!

Julian James 16692-084
Po Box 1027
Coleman, Florida 33521

FB: Julian Jamaica Tha Author James
IG: Jamaicadiddat
Text #: 208-225-4018

Jamaica

Chapter 1

~Jae~

I parked my car and got out slamming the door behind me. The bitch had left the front door wide open, so I just walked in as I pinned my hair up into a ponytail.

"MiMi," I called, but she didn't answer.

I closed the front door and turned around only to be face-to-face with Ashanti holding a gun. "Yeah, bitch!" she yelled, feeling powerful with the gun aimed at me. Her hands were shaking, and I knew the bitch was scared.

"Where's, MiMi?" I asked, but her eyes didn't leave my stomach. "Huh?" I snapped my fingers toward her.

"Stop! Fuckin'! Movin'!" She steadied the gun at my head. "You pregnant?"

I stopped walking, frustrated that I gave Trap my piece. '*Fuck*!' I screamed inside. I'd never been without protection.

"Bitch, you're pregnant," she answered the question herself. "Rocket, just had to have you, huh?" She kept going.

"Yeah!" I snapped my neck and cracked my knuckles. Fuck her and that pistol. I've gotten hit up before. "MiMi!" I yelled again ready to leave 'cause the bitch wasn't about to do shit but run her fucking mouth.

"Jae," MiMi came limping down the stairs.

Knowing that her bitch ass mother hurt her caused me to spazz out. "Bitch, I'm 'bout to fuck you up!" I charged at Ashanti.

A loud, sudden sound made me stop in my tracks.

Jamaica

Chapter 2

~Rocket~

I watched the paramedics load Goon into the ambulance from afar.

"How he doin'?" asked Brad.

"Little nigga is a G. He's gonna make it," I informed him. The police were wrapping the yellow tape around the place, near Mayo's dead body. "Man, that shit happened so fast, yo." A nigga had to stay ready for war at all times. "It's all good, our nigga still breathing. The enemy is dead!" I said.

"True story," he replied.

I dialed Jae's number, keeping my eyes on the pigs.

"Hello?" It wasn't Jae who answered. The voice was of someone hysterical. I started moving towards Brad's ride with my brows knitted. "

Who's this?" I asked.

"Daddy, it's MiMi."

"What's wrong, baby girl?"

"No!" someone screamed in the background.

"MiMi!" I barked.

"Mommie shot Jae!" she screamed. I froze dead in my tracks. My heart stopped beating as MiMi repeated her words even stronger, *"Mommie shot Jae!"*

"No—no, my baby!" I cried out.

Jamaica

Chapter 3

~Trap~

Muthafuckaz thought shit was a game, but with a team like ours, niggaz realized real quick we were not to be fucked with, not even in church. I smirked at the look Mayo had on his face while I was standing over him emptying the clip. Bitch made ass nigga had that surprise look like, '*Where the fuck did this nigga come from?*' Real niggaz move in silence at all times.

"Fuck you!" I spat at the pussy ass nigga as I finger fucked the trigger.

I was still heated with myself on the inside because I had to leave Rocket, my brother, by himself with Goon. I knew my bro wanted me gone 'cause I was on the run and Rocket damn sure wasn't going to leave the little nigga's side until help got there. Rock-solid and G'd the fuck up, that's the type of nigga he is.

"Fuck!" I dropped the hammers at my feet only to see fresh red bloodstains on my all-white dope mans. Pussy ass nigga thought he caught us slipping laying our goons to rest, only to be left slumped up by a real shotta. The vibration of my cell phone pulled me back to time. "Hello," I answered with a smile on my face.

"How are you, sexy?"

"Good, now that I'm talking to you." I let my gangsta side go when I'm vibing with my baby girl. Lil momma brings the pudding side out of a nigga.

"Is that always going to be your line for me?" she asked, I could hear that huge smile that I love so much in her tone.

"You should already know the answer to that, baby, "I used my best Patwha voice. "Right?" I continued.

"Yeah, you're right—" she paused. "Where is my sister?" she questioned me switching the tone in her voice.

"She just left me to go get, MiMi." I sat straight up on the sofa to get the remote, so I could turn the monitors on and could view the spot. Lil' momma's worried tone had me on my toes. "Why you ask?" I picked one of the hammers up off the floor only to see Jae's pistol in my hand. '*Damn, she never bounced anywhere without a banger,*' I thought.

"Because someone answered her—"

"What!" I cut her off.

"Someone answered her phone?"

That couldn't be, Rocket was still at the church. I was already in the garage getting ready to enter the Audi. "Talk to me, Chessan!" I snapped.

Her breathing was so heavy I felt it in my own chest. "And they were screaming, then they hung up on me!" she screamed.

I hung up on her and dialed Rocket's number as I backed out into the street. "Come on, bruh answer ya joint, B," I spoke into the phone mashing the gas pedal to the floor. I got Rocket's voicemail, so I hit redial. "Fuck!" I cussed myself even more for letting Jae bounce by herself without me or her hammer after what we had just encountered in the church.

"Yo' son," Rocket answered. "I'm on my way to Ashanti's spot." I relaxed easing my foot up off the gas pedal. "That bitch shot, Jae!" he said that in one breath.

I dropped the phone, shaking my muthafuckin' head as my foot rammed the pedal to the mat.

Chapter 4

~Jae~

I was born to lose but this bum bitch didn't know I was built to win. The second I saw the pistol in the hoe's hand, I knew shit was 'bout to get real. Fuck all that, though. I'll never let a nigga or bitch, much less a bum bitch, intimidate me, just 'cause she got a burner in her possession.

Boom!

The loud sudden sound caused me to stop moving, but I was still alert and thinking faster than ever. I tossed the phone in MiMi's direction without turning around. I had to keep my eyes on this bitch. No part of my body burned so I knew that the hoe didn't hit me up. I ran my hand down my stomach just to make sure I wasn't hit. Still showing no sign of fear in front of this sketal. I'll die standing on my feet with a smile on my face.

"Mommie, no!" MiMi wailed. I knew MiMi was crying and scared at the same time. Her voice trembled with fear.

"Take ya muthafuckin' ass back upstairs, now!" Ashanti yelled. The way she talked to MiMi had my head and body on fire.

The shotta in me wanted to just rush the bitch, but I knew I couldn't. A scared person will kill faster than a real muthafucka. I turned my full body around and faced MiMi. She had my phone in her hand.

"Just go upstairs, baby." I talked to her in the softest voice ever. "Everything is going to be okay."

She looked at her mom with pure hate before she locked her eyes on me. "You promise?" she questioned me. Her little body was trembling. "Promise me everything is going to be okay, Jae?"

Jamaica

The rude gal in me spoke up, "I promise you that." She tilted her head to the side. My word was all that I had, and I had to make her feel it. "On my life, everything is going to be alright. I can promise you that!"

Watching MiMi limping up the stairs brought pain to my soul. Never in my life would I do anything to hurt my child. Never. Once baby girl was out of sight, I turned back around to face Rocket's dumb ass baby mother. All that fuck shit Rocket used to spit about letting Ashanti live, went out the bloodclot window with me today.

"Dat a weh yuh duh now?" I had to stop myself before I continued cause her dumb ass didn't understand Patwha. "So, this is what you do now?" I cleared my throat. "You beat on your child knowing she can't defend herself?" I cracked my knuckles, pulling my tears back for MiMi. To get Rocket's attention, this dumb bitch took her pain and anger out on their child. Today was the day that I had ran out of patience with this sketal.

"What the fuck I do over here—" She waved the gun around the room in the air. "—is my fucking business. And the last time I checked—" She lifted her shirt up showing me her stomach. "I pushed her out!"

"And what the fuck that mean?" Muthafuckas didn't realize that birthing a child didn't make them a mother. I knew that first-hand, my mother gave birth to me but my grandmother mothered me. I took off walking toward Ashanti again, I wanted this over and done with.

Boc! The bullet whisked past my ear causing my eardrum to explode.

I was fuming on the inside this bitch was playing with my life with a hammer. "What the fuck?" I snapped. "Bitch if you gonna wet me up do that shit and get it over with." But I knew better, Ashanti wasn't 'bout that life. It caused me to laugh, she knew she wasn't shit even though she had the hammer in her hand.

"You think shit is a game, huh?" she barked.

"Yeah, bitch! Everything 'bout you is a game," I replied. "Put that hammer down and square up. Show a bitch what you got," I challenged her.

Lines formed in her forehead and I knew that hoe was thinking. Seconds passed and neither one of us moved. "You ain't said shit." She tossed the burner on the sofa.

Without thinking about my baby or my life. I bolted toward that bitch like a flash of lightning with thunder behind me. *Bam*! Her fist connected with my nose causing me to stagger way the fuck back. I twisted my nose feeling every bit of the punch. Before I had a chance to regroup, the bitch kicked me and landed a punch to my temple. The kick stunned me more than anything. The room spun and before I knew what was happening, I felt my body going down.

"What now bitch?" was the last thing I heard from Ashanti before I clocked out.

Jamaica

Chapter 5

~Rocket~

Ain't no muthafuckin' way that bitch done shot my fuckin' wife? The Ashanti I knew wasn't 'bout that gunplay at all, but I assumed she was tired of them ass whoopings from Jae.

"Where ya ride, B?" I asked Brad looking over the parking lot waiting on him to show me a signal.

The moment his hand went up, I took off. All Ashanti knew how to do was pop her fuckin' gums a hundred miles per hour. But replaying MiMi's screams in my head caused my heart to palpitate and my feet to move faster.

"Fuck!" I banged the car door shut. "Where the keys at, son?" I questioned Brad trying my hardest to keep calm and not have a fuckin' heart attack.

I couldn't lose my wife and our baby. *Fuck! Hell no!* Jae always kept her strap on her, I recalled, and the thought alone caused me to relax a little. Maybe MiMi had phrased it all wrong and maybe she didn't.

"Fuck!" All kind of thoughts ran through my head.

"You straight, my nigga?" Brad quizzed with a puzzled look as he handed the keys over to me.

The boyz in blue placed yellow tape all around the church. "Hell yeah," I said praying on the inside that everything was peace with my wife, our unborn child, and MiMi. I prayed as I cleared us out of the parking lot.

I hit Jae's line back to back, but I kept getting her voicemail. *Relax, Ashanti ain't 'bout that life.* I took a deep breath, holding my phone in my hand and mashing the gas pedal to the mat.

Jamaica

My phone rang in my hand and for a split second I thought it was Jae until I saw the name on the screen. "Yo' son," I answered, then gave Trap the details about Jae. "That bitch done shot, Jae!"

Chapter 6

~Trap~

I wasn't even thinking about the pigs clocking me for speeding. Today wasn't the day for them to be fucking with me, real talk. I held my toolie on my lap with one in the chamber ready to blast a hole straight through a muthafucka's head. TTG, that's how I was at all times; *Trained To Go*! As I turned on Ashanti's block, I noticed Jae's car parked right in front of Ashanti's crib. I pulled to the other side of the street and cut the engine. I tucked my hammer under my black tee shirt into my jeans. Before I could exit the car, I heard tires screeching behind me.

    I leaped out of the car removing my joint from my waist. My momentum was already on a stack, along with my trigger finger ready to fuck the trigger away. Fuck a nigga trying to catch me slipping. I'd be damn if I go out by myself. Every time a real nigga leaves this earth, two bitch made niggas must be on their way to. Spotting Rocket's face behind the wheel, I easily stashed the heater back on my waist. Then looked around the neighborhood, I didn't see anyone out and about. Brad was posted up in the passenger seat.

    "Alright, my nigga. I'm good from here!" Rocket yelled to the little young nigga as he exited the ride.

    "You sure?" he asked getting out the car meeting Rocket at the hood.

    "Yeah, B," I answered. "He good." I was few steps behind my brother.

    Rocket stepped briskly and I couldn't even imagine what that nigga was thinking at a time like this. Hoping for the best was always my number one thought but knowing that dirty bitch called *life*. I knew shit could be worse of the worse behind Ashanti's front door.

Chapter 7

~Jae~

Everything that happens in this life is either a gift or a curse and the feeling of being defeated feels like more than a curse. The atmosphere strikes me badly like death is banging at my bloodclot front door with its arms wide open, ready to swallow me whole.

"Argghhh," a moan escaped from my mouth in a whisper.

Pain struck me all over, but I refused to just give up and let this pussy clat sketal beat me out of life.

"What now, bitch?" Ashanti's last words reiterated in my head.

The thought of seeing her dead by my hands pushed me to get the hell up fast. But with the pain, I just couldn't. "Argghh, my baby." I panicked and every joint that hurt on my body, I pushed to the very back of my head as I open my eyes. Life over death. I could hardly see shit, the room was dark. "Damn." Lifting my hands up to wipe my eyes even hurt. "Weh deh bloodclot?" I mumbled. "What did that bitch hit me with? Fuck all that, I'm 'bout to push through this shit," I coached myself.

Using all the strength that I could find, I slowly pulled my upper body up. My head was spinning and throbbing, badly.

Boom! Boom! Boom! I heard someone banging.

"Lawd, nuh mek meh guh dun like des ya," I said a prayer asking God not to let me die like this.

"Open this muthafuckin' door, Ashanti," Rocket's voice boomed, and nothing ever sounded better than his voice.

He was the pain reliever to mu soul. *Boom! Boom!* I could hear the door cracking and the hinges breaking.

"Let me shoot that muthafucka, bruh?"

"Naw, son."

Just knowing that he was on the other side made me feel safe. Not even the distance mattered. But where the hell was Ashanti? Was MiMi still hurting? I utilized the sofa to help me pull my body up. Pain shot from my back to my toes, but giving up now, would only make things harder for me to start over from the floor.

"That nigga just had to come save you, huh?" I heard her voice so clear that I stopped breathing.

I didn't feel or see the crazy bitch, but I knew she was posted up nearby. *Boom!* The front door snapped open slowly and seeing some light, I collapsed face down.

"What the fuck?" Rocket's voice roared. I took a deep breath feeling his hands on me. "Baby, talk to me." He rolled me over and every pain I felt left my body with his touch. He was my cure. My medicine. My lover. My man. My protector on earth. My king, my everything. The light came on and I spotted Trap standing on the other side of me shaking his head, but Ashanti's voice clapped like thunder.

Chapter 8

~Rocket~

"Why you couldn't chase me like you chased this bitch?" She pointed the hammer at Jae. Hatred boomed from her heart and out of her mouth as she spat venom toward my wife.

"Naw, bruh, let me handle this." I caught a glimpse of Trap reaching for his hammer. His eyes asked me if I was sure.

I nodded my head. "Chase you?" I had to laugh before I placed my eyes down at my queen. Even though Jae had some bruises on her face, Lil momma was still muthafuckin' sexy. Shit like this made me love and adore her way more. She rode for me no matter what the price was. It was team Rocket from day one with Jae. "Chase you? Bitch, you done lost ya muthafuckin' mind."

I stared that hoe dead in her eyes. I wanted her to feel that same damn hate that she had for Jae from me. "You had a yateh when you had me, *bitch*!" I emphasized bitch so hard that it tasted foul when it rolled off or my tongue. "You burnt that ride and the only reason I let you walk is because you gave birth to my seed."

Her hands trembled with the pistol, but the Ashanti I knew didn't pop nothing but bubble gum. She didn't have the heart to make that muthafucka smoke, especially at me. I picked Jae up and my nigga reached out to help me, not taking his eyes off Ashanti. I welcomed his help with a tap on his shoulder. Ashanti stepped back shaking her head as hot tears danced on her face.

"All I ever wanted from you—" She took a deep breath. "—was a family!" she screamed.

I knew if I didn't get Jae out of the house fast, it would later haunt me, forever. "Bruh, take her to the car," I whispered to Trap.

"And leave you?" Trap questioned.

"You have to handle this for me."

He didn't question me anymore. What was understood didn't need to be explained. He threw Jae over his shoulder and stepped backward toward the doorway.

"Why Rocket—why?" The pistol danced from one hand to the other as she wiped tears away watching Trap exit the house with Jae.

"Where is, MiMi?" Fuck her emotions, feelings, heart, and soul. Fuck her all the way together. This bitch was nothing to me.

"Why Rocket?" She steadied the gun on me.

"Where is my daughter, Ashanti?" I rubbed my temple slowly, trying my hardest to keep calm, but that notion was on its way out the door.

"That's all you are worried about?"

I suspected that she was jealous of, MiMi but today she made it clear that she was jealous of her own seed. "What about me, Rocket?"

I walked straight up to her. The gun rested on my chest. "Where is my seed at, shorty?"

She gripped the gun with both hands. "Fuck that little bi—"

Whap! Before she could even finish the sentence my right hand was already across her face as my left-hand grad hold of the pistol. I snatched the hammer from her. *Bop*! I gun butted that bitch's forehead. Her body staggered backward but I gripped her by her shin snatching her ass forward. Her eyes pleaded for help, but help was nowhere near. This ass whopping was overdue. This was for the old and new headaches that the bitch gave me. I tucked the gun in my waist. Blood oozed from her lips and nose as I tried to choke the life out and some sense into the dumb bitch.

"Ashanti, where the fuck is my child?" I said through clenched teeth. Ashanti's eyes danced in the back of her head, so I eased my grip up from her neck. "Say sumthing, bitch!" But my words fell on deaf ears. "MiMi!" I yelled out hoping my baby girl would run downstairs, but nothing happened. Fearing the worst, I snatched Ashanti's fake ass hair in my hands, jerking her head and body forward. "Bitch, don't let me toe tag you, yo'." Her eyes blinked. "Where is my daughter?"

She had yet to utter a word that I wanted to hear. I dragged her ass across the room as we climbed the stairs. "Rocket, I'm so sorry," she finally spoke as we reached the last step.

"MiMi!" I yelled again, but nothing.

I slammed Ashanti's body dead into the wall. A picture of MiMi fell to the floor as her body bounced forward. "Oh my, God. Forgive me!" she screamed.

My heart raced. I choked up thinking about my child and what her bitch ass mother could have done. "Ashanti," I begged letting my grip go as her body slid down the wall. I dropped with her. "Where is, MiMi?" Tears ran from my eyes like they were in a race to see how many it would take to soak my shirt up. I couldn't lose my seed, I just couldn't. A parent wasn't supposed to bury their innocent child. "Ashanti!" I yelled snapping that bitch's arm. "Where is, MiMi?"

"Argghh," she hollered out in pain. "I'm so sorry, Rocket," was all she said.

Then I spazzed the fuck out.

****

"Trap," Jae whispered. "Where is, MiMi?"

I eased her in the back seat, pulling my phone out of my pocket. "Relax, Shotta."

"Where is, Rocket?" her voice cracked with emotions.

My nigga Rocket loved Jae she is his world, right or wrong. Shotta was riding and asking questions later. She was his Queen and he damn sure was her King, hands down.

"Mom, you have to come over to Ashanti's house, now."

"What happened?" she asked but I knew she would be on the way.

"Mom, just get here!" I ended the call in her ear. Jae grabbed her stomach and for the first time in a long time, I watch fear dance over her face. "Shotta, everything gonna be straight." I tried to ease her mind. "Just relax."

She looked weak and tired. "Go get Rocket and MiMi!" Her tone came from deep within.

I slammed the car door shut and dashed back toward Ashanti's front door. "Rocket!" I hollered out getting nothing but silence. I looked around the first floor seeing nothing, but blood spots gracing the stairs. Twenty-five cent sizes of blood spots graced the stairs. "Fuck!" I moved faster, I spotted a body at the top of the stairs curled the fuck up in fetal position with a picture frame on the floor. Ashanti, damn, I watched her body rise and fall. Shorty was still breathing, but her face was fucked up. She was staring up at me.

"Rocket?" I yelled stepping into the bathroom.

"Yo," he finally shouted back. "I'm in the room on the left," his voice sounded weak.

Walking past Ashanti's body still on the floor gave me an eerie feeling cause I knew a bitch like Ashanti wasn't going to stop until something horrible happened. Ashanti had dragged Rocket's name and reputation through the muthafuckin' mud, but it didn't stop my nigga from loving and caring for his seed.

He was a real nigga and a damn good father. Clothes were spewed all over the room like a nigga had run-up in the bitch on a lick mission. Rocket was seated on the edge of the bed with his arms curled around a small body. My feet couldn't move. My legs wouldn't allow me to. When his face turned to meet mine, I saw death in his eyes as tears cascaded down his face.

"Fuck!" he bellowed.

I felt the walls closing in on us.

Jamaica

Chapter 10

~Rocket~

I searched upstairs with my heart at my feet. Sweat dripped from my forehead, my armpits stuck to my shirt as I tore each room apart looking for my baby girl. When I entered Ashanti's room, my heart was pounding to the max. I had faced death head-on boldly, but there was no way I could face my child dying and I was still alive and breathing. I looked under the bed, *nothing*. Fear gripped my soul as I reached out to turn the knob on the door to the closet.

"God, please let my daughter be alive," I prayed out aloud. "Don't do me like this," I begged.

Click! MiMi's body was curled up. Her hands and feet were bound separately and a washcloth was stuffed inside her mouth. Her eyes brightened when she saw my face, but I knew deep down my baby girl would never be the same. Her face was swollen and her eyes were bloodshot red. I dropped to my knees, pulled the cloth out of her mouth, then untwined each section that held her hostage. I spotted Jae's phone beside MiMi, I picked it up and stuffed it in my pocket.

"Daddy's here," I preached. Tears poured down my face onto hers.

"Daddy," she whispered. It's a sound I'll never erase from my mind, or forget.

"Shhh." I picked her up, cradled her in my arms and placed soft kisses all over her face.

How could a mother do this to their daughter? Fuck that to a child, their child. Thinking about how the bitch that gave birth to me did me, had me feeling on the edge to send Ashanti beside that bitch. I begged Jae to go to the hospital, but Lil'

Momma didn't want to hear shit from me. Stubborn should've been her name. I was so glad Miss Judith had showed up.

"Take her to the crib for me, bruh."

"Say no more," Trap said before he pulled off from me and his mom.

MiMi was still resting in my arms as we rode in the back seat of Miss Judith's truck. How could Ashanti do this to our child? A child that she carried for nine months. My tears had yet to stop.

"What are you going to do, Rocket?" Miss Judith asked interrupting my thoughts. She glanced at me through the rearview mirror.

I stared down at MiMi, thanking God I got there on time to save my seed, my woman and our unborn child. I raised my head up, shaking it from side to side. It wasn't what I was going to do, cause I knew MiMi would never forgive me if something bad happened to her mom by my hands. But the Jae that I fell in love with was not letting this shit slide off the table without revenge.

Chapter 11

~Jae~

Trap informed me that MiMi was okay but swollen. *Swollen?* The word tore my soul and reopened each bruise on my body as my heart ripped into pieces. The pain I felt earlier didn't compare to what I was feeling now. Ashanti's hands were supposed to be loving and caring, but, yet they had caused pain to her own blood. A child that I fell in love with and would do anything for. There's no way in hell, Ashanti's gonna rest in peace on earth with me still breathing.

"Min uh care wah mi ave feh lose feh dat sketal feh feel wah, MiMi afeel now," I said through clenched teeth.

"Sis, let me take you to get checked out," Trap's voice disturbed my thoughts.

I didn't care what I had to lose for that bitch Ashanti to feel what MiMi was feeling. "I'm good, bruh." I knew they had doctors on call, but I didn't need shit but Ashanti's head. I repositioned myself in the back seat, I needed to sit up. I rubbed my stomach, smiling down at my baby budge. "Yuh a bam irmah a wicked world, but as long as mi a live, mi a guh guard yun Weh mi life." My pledge to my child, this world is wicked but as long as I was breathing, I was going to guard him or her with my life. "My phone." I reached for it, remembering that I tossed it to MiMi in the house.

"Where is it?" Trap asked.

"Innah that bitch's house."

"Fuck!" He clapped back.

"Call Rocket," I demand.

Damn, I shouldn't have been so damn mean to Rocket, but if he had just let me tag that bitch months ago, this wouldn't be happening right now. "Fuck!" Frustration hit me hard. "Bruh, Shotta's line at ya baby mama's spot."

Baby mama, that bitch ain't nothing but an egg carrier. A mother don't take their stress and frustration out on their child.

"Oh, word—" he paused. "—that's what's up." He stopped responding and I had to wonder what Rocket was spitting in his ear. "A'ight, hold on." Trap handed me the phone. I stared at it for a few seconds before I took it from his hand.

This was not a good time for me to be at war with my husband. My vow-wedding ring danced on my finger reminding me of the vows I said and took, for better or worse, in sickness and in health, till death do us part.

"Hello."

"Baby," his voice trembled, not with fear but from hurt, my heart stopped. He's my armor and when he is hurting, I'm hurting too. "I got ya phone." His breathing was way off, a breathing that I'd never heard before.

I was already weak, but hearing his tone crushed my soul. "How is she?" Tears splashed down my face as I asked him about MiMi.

"Good,"

I smiled. "She's a G just like us."

Us a family that that dumb bitch Ashanti tried to destroy. A family that would forever be. It will always be me and not her. Always us, never them.

"Gotti got a doc waiting," he continued. "Come with us, Jae," he begged.

"Rocket," I had to get my emotions under control, but I couldn't. "I'll be home waiting on y'all, I am fine." I ended the call.

A few bones on my body ached, that was that. My head thumped and that was nothing I couldn't shake off. Ashanti caught me all the way the fuck off guard. This wasn't just a beef between us anymore, it was war. This would be the only time that bitch thought she won a fight with me.

Jamaica

Blood Stains of a Shotta 3

Chapter 12

~Rocket~

How the fuck is all this shit happening to my baby girl. I declared to be her protector and I'd failed. Failed to protect her from harm.

"Draymond—" Miss Judith placed her hands on my shoulders. "—some things we can't change or prevent." Watching the doc and his team care for MiMi warmed my heart but my soul had death written all over it for Ashanti. "And no, that is not the way to handle Ashanti, either." I had to glance at Miss Judith. She'd read my thoughts without me saying a word. "What she did—" she carried on. "—will kill her slowly but fast, itself."

"Why?" I dropped my head feeling defeated.

"I can't give you the answer to why she did what she did. But what I can say is this," I picked my head up to face her. "When a woman is hurt to the point of no return, there is nothing she won't do to prove her point."

"Hurt?" I asked confused. I never hurt Ashanti even when that bitch did the most.

"Yes, hurt. You are no longer with her. You moved on and married Jae. You are happy." She smiled. "You're going to be a father, again. Her hurt turned into hate and when that is planted, jealousy evolves into evil."

I shook my head, there's no way she was ever getting MiMi again. *Fuck outta here, I should've snapped her neck.* After sitting for some uncounted minutes without saying a word, the doctor approached us. I stood to my feet watching my daughter laying on the bed talking to the nurses.

"Mr. Wallace." He extended his right hand out to me and I reached back. "I'm, Doctor Blair, sorry to meet under these circumstances." I nodded my head. "Your daughter is going to be okay. She has no broken bones." I felt a little bit of relief, but I was still hurt from not being there to protect her. "The bruises, however, are going to cause some swelling. I will prescribe her some medicine nothing too hard for a child her age."

"Okay." Miss Judith was at my side. "How long will it be before she can leave?" I asked hoping for the best.

"Her X-Rays came back—" he paused, and I held my breath. "No broken bones," he said, and I thanked the Man above, as I waited on Doc to continue. "She is good to go home from here."

"Doc," I gripped his hands. "Thank you."

"It's my job," he reminded me and with that, he left the room.

I walked over to my baby girl and moved her hair out of her face. "How's Daddy's princess feeling?" I said picking her up in my arm as I placed soft kisses all over her face. I hoped my kisses would ease the pain and the hurt that her mother had caused.

"I just want to go home with you and Jae."

"Your wish is my command, baby girl."

****

~Trap~

Telling Chessan, Jae's sister, what had gone down was hard, but I had to tell her, she kept blowing down the phone. Shorty was flipping the fuck out on the phone as I told her what I knew had happened.

"Where she at?" she questioned.

"Resting."

"Trap, yuh nuh play wi meh." Her accent was out and heavy. "Put meh bloodclot sista pan deh phone meh youth."

That shit turned me the fuck on. I had to grab my dick to keep it from swelling the fuck up in my jeans. "Chessan, you not listening to me," I based my voice up. "She is sleeping, and I'm not gonna wake her up."

"It nuh pussyclath matta, meh on meh way deh!" she yelled. "And I'ma see you!" She switched the languages up hanging the phone up on me.

I was glad that she was on the way back to the states. I couldn't wait to tame that tongue with this dick when she landed in Brooklyn. If she was just a female I was hitting and didn't care about, I would have went off, but lil' momma was mad special to my heart.

Jamaica

Chapter 13

~Jae~

When Rocket arrived home with MiMi, he asked Miss Judith could she get MooMoo from her mother for him. As always, Miss Judith did whatever for them boys. Her love for Rocket and Trap was of measurable worth. I pushed my pain to the back burner as I catered to MiMi before she fell asleep.

"Jae." Rocket grabbed my arm as I was walking past him. "Thank you." He handed me my phone.

"It's nothing to thank me for, it's my job." I looked up at him. "I told you from day one, I'ma ride with you no matter what. I'm cut up for this shit with you."

He jerked his head up and down. "Always us—" he paused.

I finished his statement, "Never them!" I wrapped my arms around his waist as he rubbed my face before touching my eye. "Ouch!" I flinched. It was still sore from Ashanti's hand. "You know I've let ya egg carrier get away with a lot of things?" I stared him straight in his eyes. "But what she did to, MiMi, today—" I paused blinking away my tears.

"Shhh." He placed two fingers on my lips. He knew what time it was.

Jamaica

Chapter 14

~Rocket~

"Aye yo', I'ma swing over to the hospital with Trap to cheek on, Goon."

Jae tipped up on her toes pressing her lips against mine. I wanted her to help me ease some of this pain and pressure away with that pussy. But I had to move and show my face to my little nigga, cause hitting that pussy, right now, would be night-night for a nigga.

"Let me know how G is," she referred to, Goon. I tasted her lips one more time before I released her from our embrace. "And if you need me, you know the rest," she said heading back to MiMi's room. Her hips swayed to its own music and her ass bounced so damn right that I had to look away.

Trap made sure to let me know that he'd told Chessan what was going on with her sister. "Shorty showed me another side of her on the phone, son."

I laughed for the first time all day. "Word?"

"B, lil' momma was spitting their language with a whole lot of gangsta in it, too."

It had been a minute since I had seen Trap this happy. My bruh was glowing and didn't even know it.

"I gotta get to that nigga Cuba, yo." I watched a jeep full of niggas out peripheral on my left side.

"I already know that B gotta find and touch that fool proper," Trap stated.

"Check ya at three o'clock hand out." I reached for my pistol.

I got a glimpse of Trap's head moving to my left side to see the jeep full of niggas beside us. The light turned red, instead of stopping dead at the light and right beside them niggas, I eased back, switching behind them. Refusing to get caught like Biggie. Trap had his burner at his fingertips. The vehicle had an NC license plate. I counted the shadows from the back window, there were five niggas. I cocked a bullet in the chamber. Here in Brooklyn, a nigga gotta be on point. The light changed, the other vehicles in the right lane moved, but the jeep didn't budge. Both my hands were already on my pistol. My left knee kept the steering wheel steady.

"What the fuck?" Trap expressed.

"Breathe easy, bruh. We have more advantage than them." I watched the brake light disappear from the jeep, then I eased off the brake myself, staying a nice distance back. "This shit is crazy, can't rest till that nigga Cuba is dead." That gangsta's money was that long, he could have anyone do his dirty work while he was laying back calling the shots. But that's not what a real gangsta Bossman does. A real muthafuckin' Boss puts that work in to. That was the real difference between us.

"Damn right! We gotta touch that nigga fast, son."

The jeep made a left on Lefferts Ave, and I kept straight. Trap pulled his NY fitted hat down but kept his toy on his lap.

"Undo this bitch." I handed my baby over to him.

He took the 9mm without saying a word. I kept my eyes all over the place as I rode. *Jay-Z's* song, *Where I'm From* was playing. I pressed the volume up as we rode to Kings County Hospital.

'Where the grams is slung, niggas vanish every summer Where the blue van would come, we throw the work in the can and run. Where the plans was to get funds and skate off the set to achieve this goal quicker sold all my weight wet faced with immeasurable odds still I get straight bets.'

****

Brad met us at the entrance of the hospital and led the way for us to Goon's room. "I told his people you were on the way," Brad said before we entered the room.

His mother and a caramel-skinned shorty were present. Shorty was at his side holding his hand.

"Rocket?" His mom stood up and greeted me with a hug.

"How is he?" My nigga had a tube coming out of his mouth. I let her go.

"The doctors say he's going to be okay." That nigga Goon looked just like her, only difference was that she was shorter. "Thank you for staying with him."

No parent wanted to bury their seed. I still had his and Ashanti's blood all over my jeans and shoes I had yet to change the shit that I had on. Brad gave me a black tee that he had in his ride at the church.

"That's nothing, if it was me, I know he would've done the same," I responded.

"That is my daughter, E'mon." I saw the resemblance right away between her and Goon. They both had butt chins, brown eyes, and flat foreheads.

"Hello."

"Hi," she said turning her head back to her brother.

I walked over to him to the opposite side of E'mon. She was pretty, a nigga couldn't deny that if he wanted to.

"Would you like it if I gave you some time with him?" She was polite.

"Naw." I looked at my nigga resting and dapped my nigga's free hand up. "My people gonna be here with him just to make sure don't nothing pop off." Shorty kept her eyes on her brother, so I looked toward his mom. "And don't worry about the bill, I got it."

E'mon's eyes stared up at me and this time I had to look away. I hit Gotti's line as I was leaving the hospital to let him alert Ice that I needed his attention at the hospital. "Consider it done, son."

Chapter 15

~Jae~

I was still a little sore from them blows that Ashanti had landed on me. I had underestimated that hoe all together. But what I had in mind for that bitch was unforgiven and unforgettable by God himself. I quietly entered the room hoping I wouldn't wake MiMi up, but I had to check up on her. Her face was swollen and that fumed my blood pressure all the way up more. How could a mother treat her child like that? I kept asking myself over and over again. Just how? I rubbed my stomach before I took a seat in the chair across the room. MiMi's body jerked, and I wondered was it from pain or a nightmare that she was having.

"No!" she screamed lifting her hand up to cover her face.

I jumped out of the chair and rushed to her side. "Baby girl." Her eyes opened. "It's okay, I'm here and no one is going to hurt you." I held her hand as I rubbed her shoulder. "You're safe now." Tears ran from her eyes onto the bed. Not knowing what else to do or say, I crawled into the bed with her. "I promise," I said as I held her in my arms rocking her back to sleep.

The vibration of my phone in my pocket woke me up. I had fallen asleep with MiMi. I easily removed myself from the bed and out of the room. "Hello," I answered as I closed the room door. "Wah gwaan mi daughta."

"Hello, Daddy," I responded walking into the kitchen to grab me a bottle of water. My mouth was hella dry. "A wah gwan up deh wid yuh?" He wanted to know what was going on with me in America. "Nutin, wah mek yuh ah ask?"

Jamaica

Chessan ended up calling our father in Jamaica telling him what had taken place between me and Ashanti. "Cause yuh sista she its ova yuh husband," his tone was harsh.

"Daddy, hold up." I grabbed the bottle from the fridge and twisted the cap open. Chessan had told him the fight was over Rocket. "Rocket didn't do anything," I slammed back. "And first of all, nuh disrespect, but don't call me talking or asking about my husband in a tone like that."

"Em up deb and feh em baby yuh fight, Jae, em nuh check 'er," he snapped.

"Yeah, I was fighting his baby mother, so fucking what!"

Chessan and my father didn't know the real deal behind the whole damn story. I made a mental note to call Chessan and cuss her the fuck out, blood or not. "Luk, weh mi duh inna feh mi house is mi business." I let him know that what I did in my house was my business, not his or Chessan. Fuck outta here with that bullshit he was spitting.

Click! Instead of disrespecting him with my words, I let him slide with my actions, the dial tone. But I knew the conversation was far from over. I was scanning through my contacts to call my sister, but Miss Judith's name and number flashed across my screen.

"Hello." I tucked the phone in the back pocket of my jeans and headed toward the door.

"What happened to ya face, Jae?" MooMoo asked the moment she saw my face.

"How are you going?" I changed the subject, watching Miss Judith shaking her head.

"Good, but what happened?" She was determined to find out. I stepped to the side letting them into the house.

"Jae, I hate to tell you, but I have some things to handle," Miss Judith said handing me a book bag belonging to Moo Moo.

"Okay, make sure you call me when you get home," I advised her.

"I will." She gave her granddaughter a hug and a kiss before she left. "You hungry?" I asked Moo Moo closing the door, dropping the bag at the door.

Moo had yet to move, she was a very strong-minded ten-year-old little young lady. I strolled toward the kitchen to find something to cook for dinner. Moo was behind me with her hands crossed over her chest.

"Take a seat." I opened the deep freezer scanning it for something to cook. Fried chicken wings had to do tonight. I took out two packs placing them into the sink as I turned the water onto them so they could defrost. I took a deep breath.

"MiMi, called me," I started telling Moo exactly what had taken place between me and Ashanti and how I ended up with the bruises on my face. "MiMi's face is a little swollen," I continued. Moo's fists closed together on the table, "But she is going to be okay."

Tears ran down her face and it rooted nothing but hate for Ashanti. "What did daddy do?" She wiped her tears away.

I knew Rocket had beat Ashanti up, but I wasn't going to disclose that. He was an angel to his girls, and I wanted to keep it that way. "He said she is not going back with her mother."

"Well, I'm staying here too, then," her tone was serious.

"Talk to your daddy when he gets in."

"I will," she said getting up from the table. "I'm going to see my sister."

****

I let the kids stay in the room as I cook dinner. Fried chicken wings, mash potatoes, green beans, and butter rolls. It was close to seven before I got done and Rocket still wasn't home. I told the girls to take a shower before they ate. They ate in the room as I cleaned the kitchen up. I saved a plate for Rocket and Trap as I ate a chicken wing with a butter roll. I didn't have the appetite to really throw down like I wanted to. I had way too much on my mind.

I took a shower and laid across the sofa waiting for Rocket to get in. The girls were in the room I heard some laughter between them, and it lifted my spirits just a little. I called Chessan, but she didn't answer. It was 8:30 when Rocket and Trap marched through the front door.

"Son, a nigga is hungry," Trap stated.

"What's new?" I add my piece.

That nigga was always hungry. They both glanced at each other and laughed.

"I'm glad you know ain't nothing new, sis," he said walking into the kitchen. "The question is, did you cook?"

I looked up at my husband and smiled. He was so damn sexy that I could really eat him for a meal. "Go get some rest. I'll be in the room in a minute." Knowing our family was safe and sound, I smiled and followed my husband's directions.

Chapter 16
Rocket

"First thing in the a.m. we're checking all the spots to make sure everything is everything," I said before taking a bite into the crispy chicken wing. "I think I'm going to let Brad step up while Goon gets some rest." Trap had yet to say a word, that nigga was working on his fourth chicken wing and third butter roll. "That little nigga Goon hardheaded, though." My brother ain't said shit. "Trap!"

"Yo'," he mumbled with a mouth full of food. "I'm listening to you, bruh." He lifted his head up from the plate.

I cracked up. "Get some rest." I fist bumped him leaving him at the table. Halfway through the room, I stopped and turned around. "I love you, my nigga!"

When I didn't have a parent to show me some love, he shared his mother with me. He gave me his word, his love, and his loyalty. "Death before dishonor, bruh. I love you, too, son!"

"Death before dishonor," I reiterated with loyalty.

We were all we had. Tray was gone but he'll always be a part of us. I peeked into the girl's room and they were fast asleep. Jae was knocked the fuck out when I entered our bedroom. I studied her body she was positioned on her left side. Her back to me, shorts and a wife-beater kept her skin from being bare. The television was on, but the sound was on mute. Her Glock was on the nightstand, right in arms reach.

I slid my shoes off and headed to the shower. As the hot water ran over my head, I couldn't help but think about my girls, especially, MiMi. I just hoped my love would cover her pain and hurt. Ashanti would have to kill me in order to have custody of our child.

Jamaica

On a different note, Cuba had to be found, fast. I had a whole damn borough to feed and run. Ro's bitch ass father, the succa that pointed the snitch finger at my father had to disappear. My father's appeal had to get done.

"Fuck!" I scrubbed my skin as the hot water washed off nothing but today's dirt.

****

My dick was already hard before I climbed into the bed, naked. Jae didn't budge. I stared at her beauty with some help from the light off the T.V. I was a lucky nigga to have her in my life. I placed stupid long wet kisses on her legs to wake her up. Every muscle in my dick jumped and throbbed.

"Awww," she moaned.

Her taste was like almonds, roasted glazed. Her breathing was slow, felt like it was coming from the soles of her feet. We both needed this. She turned on her back, spread her legs apart and sat up to face me.

"Naw, let me do that for you." I stopped her from taking off her shirt.

I leaned in and tasted her lips before lifting her shirt up over her head. Her breasts stood still, they were firm. Motherhood had her plump and I was loving every bit of it. Her nipples swelled as I licked each one. She clamped my head with both hands as I leaned her head back onto the bed. I slowly pulled my head from one tilt to the next. I sucked each one like a strawberry.

"Rocket," she sobbed but I ignored her.

She was mine, her heart, body, and soul had Draymond Wallace written over them. Each gulp that I took, her body jerked as I nibbled on each nipple. I took a mouth full of her ass through the shorts. I glanced up at her with the pussy in my mouth, her head twisted from side to side.

"Rocket," she groaned, I heard the agony in her voice.

I let my face drop on her pussy for a second taking in her scent as my tongue dance a little on her clothing. I knew she was soaking wet I felt the moisture on my chin. I was nose deep and chin deeper. I used my hands to move her clothes as my body rested on the bed with my face on her cat. This would be my dinner it was the only meal that could fill me up. I eased her legs over my shoulders as my hands gripped her waist holding her in place.

"Oh, my God!" she huffed and puffed. "Rocket." I pushed my tongue deep as my nose rubbed on her clit. "Rocket, please," she begged, but it all fell on deaf cars. She was soaking wet and I couldn't wait to quench my thirst. I blew air in her and sucked it right back out. "Fuck!" she yelled.

I hoped she wouldn't wake the house with her noises. My mouth danced over her clit, with each lick, I pinched the inside of her thighs with my teeth. Her legs dance under me uncontrollably. I wanted her to explode. I needed to drink from her fountain, only her juices could charge me up. Her legs held my head so tight that it pushed me to swallow that pussy, whole.

"Draymond!" Her body shook and somehow her hands grabbed my head pushing it deeper. I wanted to suck her soul out. I used my lips to hum on her clit as my tongue worked the hole. "Baby," she whispered. "Baby, I'm—" That drove me over the edge.

Her body stopped moving, her hands released my head, her legs dropped, and I knew my mission was complete. I laid there enjoying the sweetness of her fruit.

Jamaica

Chapter 17
~Jae~

I swear to God, after a nut like that I didn't have the strength in me to move from his head game, but I had to. My husband was a beast at commanding my body to explode in ways that I couldn't even explain. I pulled him up to me by his head and he complied. His dick hit my thing and I caught my breath in my chest. I'd kill a bitch over him, smoke as many niggas with him and for him. Rob a bank if he needed me to. Run up in a prison blasting if they had him. I would give him my last breath to live if he needed it. That's how much I love this nigga. I moved my legs apart welcoming him to lay his pipe as I lean up to taste my juices on his lips, his mouth and tongue.

"Argghhh." I bit his bottom lip as he entered me, "Keep it right here." He stopped moving and I wrapped my legs around him. "Yassssss," I said still holding onto his mouth. My hands gripped his back pulling him deeper into me where he belonged. He pulled his mouth from me resting it in the cape of my neck, sucking and biting my flesh. During each thrust he gave me, I dug my nails deeper into his back. "Ohhh, my God." I sucked his collar bone.

"Unwrap ya legs, yo'!" he demanded and I obeyed. He man-handled himself up off me pinning my hands behind my head.

"Weh deh bloodclath?" He was blowing my mind, wild. He used one of his hands to hold mine back and used the other to lift my left leg over his shoulder with his dick still in me. "Rocket," I whined as he worked himself deep and deeper.

"That's my name, Mrs. Wallace."

"Stop!" But he knew me better, so he didn't. He picked the pace up going deeper hitting every organ inside of me. "Rocket!" I looked up at him, not wanting him to stop all that he was doing. I was near the end again. I couldn't help but close my eyes and enjoy the ride to another nut.

"Throw that pussy to me, ma," I heard him but I couldn't do nothing but tighten my muscles around his dick as I flooded him with another round of my juices. He had won another round of pure bliss.

"Let me get on top." I pulled myself together. "Please." I had to put in some work like he had done.

He came down on me still grinding away as he released my hands. I removed my legs holding onto his body as he flipped me on top of him all the while not coming out of me. I swerve my hips from side to side trying to catch my breath. His hands pulled me down on him as his mouth found my breasts and I rode him.

I picked up the pace, then slowed it down. "Damn!" escaped from his mouth. I pushed him back planting my hands on his chest for support as I rode him. Up, fast, down, slow, up, slow, down and fast. His hands slapped my ass and I worked my hips faster. "I love you!" I let him know. "This will always be your safe place." I gripped him harder. I went down covering his mouth with mine as I continue to bounce. I rode him like a bicycle, knees down and arms out.

"Jae," he said. I stopped, I didn't want him to cum so I got up off the wood. "Why, you do—"

I cut him off, "Shhh." I kissed him.

He'd made me suffer good, so it was my time to return the favor. I straddled him from the back holding his legs. I was his rider in them streets, but in these sheets, I was his bloodclath dancehall queen. Facedown with his legs apart, my upper body was between them. I felt his legs shaking and I knew exactly what time it was, but I didn't want him to tap out like that. I twisted around on it, facing him. His head was nestled into the pillow.

"Babe," he uttered. I got up off him, replacing my pussy with my mouth. I didn't need these juices to go to waste, I was already pregnant. I needed these vitamins down my throat badly. "Arrgggghh!" His hands pushed my head faster up and down his dick. His legs buckle, locking my body under his. "Fuck," he mouthed, letting his cum go as I swallowed it all. I sucked the head slow as he let me go. I was looking up at him, his body jerked, and I tighten my grip around the head not letting a drop of sperm escape. "Got damn!"

"You ready for round three, Mr. Wallace?" I said sucking and beating him back to life.

"You ain't said shit, baby," he replied smiling.

This pussy was ready for the ride.

Jamaica

Chapter 18
~Rocket~

"Wake that ass up, son." I pulled the blanket over my shoulder running from the cold air. "Baby, get up, its five o'clock."

I had told Jae last night to make sure I was up at five. "Pussy got a nigga not wanting to get up, I see," her smartass mouth chirped.

I couldn't help but chuckle. "Yeah, but that pussy was running and begging for mercy last night." My eyes were still closed but I knew she had a smirk on her face.

"Rocket, tek yuh time, memba mi pregnant," Jae mocked. I opened my eyes to see her standing at the end of the bed with a tray in her hand. "What the hell ever," I said.

She laughed handing me the tray. "Whatever, mi youth, mi dash way dem clothes, tu," she replied, then she was gone.

God had created her just for me. Shorty was that and muthafuckin' more to me. She always fucked a nigga good and to sleep, always bussing her pistol for me and with me. Made sure my dirty laundry was always trashed properly. Treat my kids like she gave birth to them, herself. Chef up the best food ever. French toast, grilled beef sausage, scrambled eggs with cheese and sliced strawberries for breakfast today with some orange juice was on my tray. I'll smoke a nigga for even looking at her. Mrs. Wallace is for my eyes only. I crushed the food within minutes, handled my hygiene, got fresh and ready to hit the streets.

"At the end of the day, yes, she is my sister, but my business should be my business to discuss. You feel me?"

Trap and Jae were having a conversation when I walked into the kitchen. "Yeah, I feel you, sis."

Jamaica

"So, all that shit, her and my daddy spitting ain't for them to understand. Cause I'll cut all this when it comes to my family, B." Her gangsta and standpoint was solid. "Smoke all dem pussyclath behind my man, straight up!

"What the fuck is going on?" I placed the tray on the table.

"Nothing, major," she responded.

"Jae," I barked.

Trap shook his head as I waited on Jae to update me.

"Long story short," she said as she took my tray up and placed my plate in the sink. "Chessan, called Wilber telling him what happened between me and ya baby ma."

"Word?"

"Yeah, so I was telling Trap." She leaned her head to the side. "They quick to run their mouths not knowing the real deal."

"Babe, don't look at it like that. She is ya sister and she's worried about you." I kissed her lips, not siding with her family, especially her father. Yes, he'd helped create her, but on the real. her grandfather was her father. "Just talk to her, Mrs. Wallace." I raised my eyebrow.

"I hear you, Mr. Wallace."

****

"Bruh, you strap?" Trap asked me as he closed the door behind him.

"Son, only time I'm freeballing is when I'm knee-deep in Jae's guts," I responded with a smile on my face thinking about last night. I pulled the .45 from my waist placing it on my left leg., "And most of the time, it's only a finger away from me, bruh." I tapped the burner pushing last night's episode to the back burner.

When I'm out in these muthafuckin' streets of Brooklyn, a nigga needs more eyes than just two. Especially ones that I can trust with my life. Having Trap was more than just a body. Son was my right-hand man, my brother. Loyalty had our bond thicker than blood. We lived by the code, loyalty over everything. Beam, my nigga that ran the Sterling Place Projects was posted up outside the building with his sister, Ta'Shonda at his side. Shorty was the bitch that Ro's snitching ass was fucking with before he got smoked by my wife. Son rocked the latest designer, red bottoms on his feet as jewelry iced his neck, wrist and fingers out.

"Life sweet I see." I dapped son up watching shorty checking me out.

"With you—" He tapped my back. "Life is great."

I released that nigga keeping eyes on his sister. Bitches couldn't be trusted. It was all about the dollar signs with hoes these days. Once that bread stopped flowing, they got mad and acted on straight emotions not remembering all the times that the moola was faithful. That's why I thanked God daily for, Jae. Island Gurl were cut from a cloth that couldn't be duplicated.

"Let me holla at you in private, B."

Ta'Shonda rolled her eyes as she walked off, but I didn't give a fuck about that bitch and her feelings.

"What's good, Boss," Beam spoke once his people were far away.

Trap was a few feet away from us with his hand under his shirt. A black Yankee's fitted hat was resting on his head.

"I'ma need some work in a few days. Shit been kinda crazy, lately." I rubbed my hands together waiting on him to continue. "Them boyz been rolling hella deep 'round this bitch—" He stopped talking as an elder couple exit the building. "Bodies dropping every day 'round this bitch, so the pigs been out, a lot deep."

"Oh, okay." I nodded my head.

"But that shit ain't stopping nothing, Bossman."

"Lay low, till shit clears up," I spoke up.

"Will do. But when I'm all the way out, I'ma need twenty Falcons flying back South for the summer."

He needed that shit bricked up. Nothing extra, straight drop. "That's all you need?"

"Yeah."

"No pressure," I added. "How am I looking?"

"Four-hunnid grand,'" he answered my question.

"Say no more." I embraced that nigga again. "My peoples will be around to collect that."

"Bet dat."

"Stay real and loyal," I preached as I walked back to my ride with Trap in tow.

Chapter 19
~Jae~

"Hmm." MiMi sat up in the bed with a huge smile on her face as she stared the plate down. "It smells so so so good."

I placed the tray in her lap and kissed her forehead. Her face was still puffed up, but I could tell the swelling was going down. "How are you feeling?"

"Better," was all she said before diving into her food. I knew she was still hurting deep inside.

"Moo." I rubbed her foot. "Good morning, sleepyhead." She had yet to move from under her blanket. "Wake and shine, lil momma."

"No," she whined.

"Alright then." I removed my hand from her foot. "Hurry up and eat MiMi, we're going shopping."

"Shopping?" Moo pulled the cover from over her head and MiMi burst into laughter. "What, shopping without me?" She sat up, glancing at MiMi eating, then settled her eyes on me. "Jae, yall leaving me?"

"Never." I handed her her breakfast. A huge smile was plastered over her innocent face. "Hurry up and eat we have a long day ahead of us." I let them know before I exited the room.

I'll always spoil my family, especially these little girls. They are my world and I was so blessed to be a part of theirs.

****

"What all we have to do today?" Moo asked as she sat her butt in the front seat of the Audi typing away on her iPhone.

Jamaica

"A lot," I replied watching MiMi strapping her seat belt on through the rearview mirror. "But I promise it's going to be all fun."

"A'ight," MiMi spoke up placing the shades I had given her over her face. "Let's hit the road, then."

"Today is going to be a great day!"

"Yes, it is," I agreed with Moo as I pulled out of the garage.

I turned the music up as we rode toward our first destination. Traffic wasn't as bad as I thought it would be, so that was a plus. Moo typed away on her phone as MiMi bobbed her head up and down staring out the window.

"What is this building?" MiMi asked when I pulled into the parking lot.

"You'll see." We parked, got out of the car and walked inside.

"Hello," I greeted the receptionist. "How are you doing?"

"Good. How may I help you?" she asked.

"I have an appointment," I said.

I had made an appointment earlier so after I gave her my name, she handed me a clipboard. "Fill it out and bring it back, please."

"No problem."

MiMi and MooMoo were already sitting in the chairs smiling away. "Are we going to see the baby, today?" MooMoo had a pamphlet in her hand from the table.

"What?" MiMi's eyes lit up like lights on a Christmas tree.

"Y'all gotta wait and see." I filled the form out attached to the clipboard watching excitement written all over their faces.

I handed the form back and took a seat. Rocket was on my mind heavy, so I took my phone out of my purse and texted him.

//: You're priceless! I don't want nothing or no one, but you and our babies. If I had to do it all over again to end up with you at the end, I'll do it in a heartbeat. I was resending Rocket's words to him along with my own thoughts.

//: Rocket, I know those streets will always be ya other main piece and I'm okay with that. I want you to know this, I'm willing to ride with you and for you at no cost in those same streets. Our family is all I have I'll die protecting our home. It will always be us and never them. On my life. Love Always, Mrs. Wallace. I pressed send.

"Mrs. Wallace," the receptionist called my name. "First door on the left."

"Let's go," I said holding each girl's hand.

Doctor Douglas and his assistant were already in the room waiting on me. "How are you doing?" he asked.

"Good," I replied leading the kids over to the chairs in the room.

Their eyes surveyed the room from top to bottom. I took my seat at the end of the wheeled cot as the assistant moved around the room. "Go ahead and lay back," Doctor Douglas directed me. I pulled my Polo shirt up to my breasts and waited. I felt the cold liquid gel as the assistant applied it on me. The girls were all smiles.

"You ready?" Doctor Douglas asked.

I closed my eyes and nodded my head. I heard the baby's heartbeat and my eyes flicked open staring at the screen.

"Wow, that's the baby!" The joy I heard in the girl's voices made me melt. They were standing up staring at the monitor.

"Are you ready to find out what you are having?"

"Yes, but MiMi and Moo, you can't tell daddy until tonight. Promise!"

Jamaica

They glanced at each other before they answered. "Promise!"

Once the baby's gender was revealed to us, the girls were super excited. They started talking about all the things we should buy the baby. I laughed at their pure happiness while expressing mine with them. The doctor smiled at our display of joy and wished us a blessed day.

Me and the girls wished him the same, then we were on our way. After leaving the doctor's office, I took the girls to get their nails and feet done.

"I can't wait to meet the baby," Moo said.

"It's my baby," MiMi added, as the Chinese lady polished her toes.

"Y'all too funny," I said enjoying our time together.

We hit Flatbush hard, stopping at almost every store buying clothes and shoes.

"Can we get daddy and uncle Trap an item?" MooMoo questioned.

"Of course, pick whatever y'all want them to have."

That they did, Cooney Island was our last stop for the day. We rode every ride together with me in the middle. We played games and won a few items. I was so happy to see the girls having fun.

"Let's get something to eat," I requested. "Cause I'm starving badly."

"The baby is hungry!" They screamed together.

"Yes!" I cracked up. "Plus me," I reminded them.

"Okay, we gonna feed you." MiMi rubbed my stomach, cracking up.

****

As soon as I started the car, the girls were out like a light. MooMoo's phone was ringing off the hook. "Hello," I answered.

"Hey, Jae," Quinta voiced. How are you doing?"

We had an okay bond, way better than Ashanti and I. "Good, Moo, is sleeping, but I'll tell her you called."

Jamaica

Chapter 20

~Trap~

//: Hit my line when you get this. I read the message Pound Cake had sent me.
//: How urgent is it? I hit back waiting on her response.
"Country, doing the damn thing over there on the Boulevard," Rocket shared his thoughts after we left Linden Blvd.
"Hell yeah," I agreed.
"How many birds you said son was pushing a week?"
"Seventeen."
"Hell yeah, he moving them birds fast."
Country was a skinny, flashy nigga, he didn't weigh no more than a buck twenty soaking wet. When we rolled up to his spot he had two pretty bitches on his arm. They rocked nothing but bras and panties.
//: It's not urgent. Just hmu when you free. ~Pound Cake~
//: How is my son? I hit right back.
"How many chickens he want this time?" I asked Rocket.
"Bruh," Rocket glanced over at me. "He said it don't matter as long as he got something to sell."
"And as long as we get that bread, we even."
"Bruh, you already know."
"Son, if that nigga don't know, he'll find out," I stated
I sat my toolie on my leg beside my phone and read Pound Cake's response *about my son.*
//: He good. ~Pound Cake~
//: And you? I had to ask.
Shorty was a good girl, she had my back ten toes down. I cared for her, but I didn't love her. I was in love with, Chessan.
//: Missing You. ~Pound Cake~

Jamaica

I ignored her statement for now, but I knew I'd have to answer it soon.

It didn't take us long to hit the last spot. Kingsborough Extension where Scarface was the nigga calling the shots. Every nigga on his team was present when we arrived.

"What's crackin' with you, Bossman?" He dapped Rocket up.

"Business," Rocket kept that shit short and straight to the point, cause some bread was missing once again from this joint.

"Already."

I kept my hands at my side, close to my strap. Yes, this was a business meeting, but niggas didn't give a fuck about principles or morals, much less loyalty. That's why I'm always strapped.

"So, shit still slackin' over this bitch," Rocket expressed at the head of the table.

A little young nigga on the left side of the table rolled his eyes, I caught his ass red-handed.

"How short is the bread, son?" Scarface dropped his head for a second before looking around at his crew. "Fifty bands."

"*Fifty bands*," Rocket repeated like he hadn't heard the nigga the first time.

I lifted my shirt, removing the hammer from my waist. This was the same problem J-Money had going on over this bitch, losing hella bread. That nigga J-Money lost his life behind that shit, along with running his muthafuckin' mouth to Shotta. My trigger finger itched, I was ready to blow some smoke.

"How much work you have left?" Rocket questioned the leader in charge.

"Five."

Rocket shook his head in his disbelief. It was so quiet you could hear a church mouse run. "Five, huh?" He looked around the room studying each face. "I need all mines by Friday. Today is Monday, so you do the math." Rocket stood to his feet.

"What the fuck?" the little young nigga that rolled his eyes barked.

Blocka! Blocka! Blocka! Niggas dashed from around the table as my hammer coughed up respect. Scarface's eyes were bulging out of their sockets.

"Y'all niggas need to learn some respect, fast. Or more bodies gonna drop." I waved my hammer around the room, staring at Scarface. "Real statement, you need to teach ya goons, respect."

Rocket smirked and headed for the door, I was right behind him. I am my brother's keeper cause I know he is mine.

Jamaica

Chapter 21

~Rocket~

Niggas stay thinking shit is a game when it comes to my money. But when I'm losing bread, throwing bricks at the penitentiary and my niggas getting slumped over loyalty, ain't nothing acceptable but death. When I first introduced myself as the new boss in charge. I made myself perfectly clear. A little means nothing to me, but loyalty means everything. I asked that you live by that at all times no matter what. If you don't know you fucking with a nigga that will definitely grant you eternal sleep. I don't just spit shit because I'm bored. I live, eat, sleep, shit and breathe death before dishonor. I'm 'bout business and money if you want to eat this is the team for you, if not you can bounce. It's all about Crown Heights, I don't rock with any other projects. So, if you're tied in with another project, take ya' self away or you'll be wiped away. The choice is yours.

"Niggas thought you was just talking, bruh." Trap added bullets to his clip. "Well, as they can see, we lay niggas down over respect."

"Muthafuckas learning right now, bruh," I said before answering my line. "Yo' what's good, B?" I kept my eyes on the road listening to the other end. "That's a bet, right there, son." The light turned red, so I stopped. Moving my eyes in all directions. "I'ma need you to swing 'round town and scoop them faces up for me." I hit the gas pedal as soon as the light changed to green. I hated sitting still at red lights. "One."

Brad updated me on Goon. My little G had opened his eyes. Ice was at his side ready to smoke a muthafucka. Since Goon was on vacation it was up to Brad to prove that he could be trusted to collect the bread from each spot.

Needing to relax, I asked, "We got enough Dutch Masters at the crib, bruh?"

"A whole damn carton, fam," he answered setting my mind at ease.

****

All three of my ladies were up waiting for me when I came through the front door.

"Daddy!" MooMoo screamed, running to me ahead of MiMi.

"My Princess." I swooped her up into my arms and rained kisses all over her cheeks. I had to enjoy it while I could because I knew she would eventually grow out of all that mushy shit.

"My turn, Moo." MiMi pulled on MooMoo's leg. "My turn."

I put MooMoo down and picked MiMi up, noticing that her face was healing better. "How's Daddy's baby doing?" I kissed both of her eyes.

"I'm happy that your here. We got a surprise for you," MiMi sounded excited.

"Who is *we*?" I asked.

"All of us," she whispered in my ear.

"Really?" I put her down, ready to find out my surprise. Trap and Moo were talking away, as Jae kept her face glued to the T.V. I walked behind her seat blocking her view with my head bending down. "Let me find out you still mad at me for beating that ting up like that last night?"

She smiled so broadly that I saw her missing tooth. "Boy, bye." She pulled my head toward her sampling my lips.

"You can pay me back later," I whispered.

"You funny." She pushed my head away laughing.

"Daddy is you ready for your surprise?" MiMi asked watching me closely.

"Ready when you are." Both my little ones disappeared out of the room. I glanced over at Jae and she shook her head like she didn't know what was going on. I kicked my shoes off and took a seat beside my wife. "How was your day?" I touched her stomach.

"I need to smoke," was her comeback.

"Don't worry Shotta, we gonna blaze for you!"

She tossed a pillow toward Trap and he smacked it to the floor. "Whateva my youth!"

The girls returned with two boxes wrapped in blue wrapping paper. MiMi sat her box down and MooMoo handed me the one she had.

"Hurry up daddy and open it!" MiMi screamed with joy.

Inside the box was a blue fitted NY hat. I placed it on my head, it was a perfect fit. Then I spotted the sonogram from the ultrasound looking up at me.

"It's a boy," I read. "*It's a boy!*" I jumped up picking both my girls up.

Jae was all smiles, Shorty was having me a boy. Trap bounced to his feet. I sat the girls down as I clapped my brother up.

"Congrats, son."

"Thank you, Uncle," I addressed him.

Jae was still smiling she hadn't moved much less to say a damn word. I stood over her. "Thank you!" I kissed her lips, bending all the way down to the floor between her thighs. I kissed her stomach. Her hands gripped my head. "Thank you!" I looked up at her.

"Naw, thank you, Mr. Wallace!" Love poured from her soul when she spoke. "I'll die making you happy," she vowed.

Jamaica

We as a family chilled watching TV. Trap left us in the living room. The girls ended up falling asleep on the sofa, so I carried each one to bed. Jae was still awake watching *Tyler Perry*.

"I love you so much," I preached to her.

"I know and it's never a one-way street, either."

I laid my head in her lap as she rubbed my waves. "Little nigga gonna look just like me," I teased.

"Don't be mad if he comes out looking just like me, son," she said with a laugh that I'll die a happy man hearing.

Trap appeared fresh and comfortable with a blunt in one hand and a bottle in the other. "Let's celebrate, bruh."

'I'm going to bed." Jae pushed me up from her lap.

"Sis, don't be mad. You'll be able to smoke and drink soon."

She flipped him off as she went to bed.

Chapter 22

~Jae~

When it came to Rocket busting his other hammer in the bedroom, I had to give him his props. He was the greatest. No one can ever be compared to him. He had me chasing dreams in broad daylight with his dick game from day one. My thugga is in a category by his damn self.

"You'll make me smoke you if you ever stop banging my back out or if you ever dick another bitch down."

He chuckled but I didn't see or find a muthafuckin' thing funny. I was serious as a heartbeat. He held me tighter as his nose rested in my hair. Our bodies were wreathed together. A fit that nothing or no one could come between.

"And I mean that shit from the bottom of my heart." I placed his hand on my chest, on my heart.

"When we took our vows—" he paused kissing my forehead. "I gave you my word, my loyalty, my heart and most of all my soul, Jae." I closed my eyes, taking our scent in. One that we had created together in love. "I'll never disrespect you or allow anyone else to." He let his hand travel until it was resting on my stomach. "Making you and our family—" he rubbed my stomach. "—happy and safe are my number one goals. Something I'll die trying to do for the rest of my days breathing on earth."

My mind, heart, body, and soul were at peace. Whatever Rocket ever decided to do life, I would be there standing, fighting and bussing whatever with him.

****

~Trap~

Jamaica

I have been blowing Chessan's phone up like a crackhead chasing his dope man. Shorty wasn't picking up, I kept getting her voicemail. Pound Cake, on the other hand, made it real clear to me that she wanted more than what we had going on. I hadn't dicked her down since I tasted some of that Island spice that Chessan fed a nigga.

"I can't give you what you really want, ma," I recalled our conversation.

"Why, Trap, why?" I heard the pain and hurt in her voice as she spoke. "You act like I'm begging you for the world!" She proclaimed bursting into tears. "I've been loving you for years," Shorty was all facts.

She'd held me down when I needed her the most. She had my back when I needed to relocate Trap Jr. Did her research for me with Wayne. Fucked me good, but she wasn't Chessan. Something about Chessan had me wanting to move to the UK saying fuck America.

"Give me a few days, I'ma see you, shorty."

She passed the phone to my son, nothing else was said. Lil' man was good, just ready to see his pops. "Hold it down for me till I get there."

"You ain't asking for nothing, daddy. I got you!"

"You ready to ride, B?" Rocket asked bringing me back to the present.

It's been days since Rocket delivered the news to Scarface about his moola, "*Have my bread by Friday!*"

"Ready when you are." I hit the blunt before passing it to him.

"You don't look too ready, son." He studied my face, but I showed nothing.

Yeah, I had a whole lot going on but when it came to me riding in them cold streets with my nigga, my brother, I was always ready. All the shit he was jaw jacking was nothing, G.

"You can skip this trip if you ain't feeling it, bruh." I knew that nigga was testing me, but he knew better.

Only death could stop me from riding with him shotgun. I tucked the gat in my waist and pulled my hoodie over my head. "Let me know when you ready, son. I lost one brother by not being there, I'll be damn if I lose this one by not being there either!"

Jamaica

Chapter 23

~Rocket~

Goon was home with his family getting his body right. "I'm ready, Boss!" Little nigga was so damn hardheaded, he reminded me so much of myself, it was mind-blowing.

The streets were his bread and jelly and his wife. I knew how he felt, cause I couldn't leave that bitch either.

"You gotta get some rest or that shit gonna cause you to lose a lot," I schooled him in front of his mother. "A fucked up mind and body frame can't protect you when bullets are flying, B." His mother excused herself before we could even continue.

"No disrespect, my nigga," I let youngin' pass with his tone. I knew he didn't mean any harm. "This is how I live!" He tapped his chest. "By the gun and I die by that muthafucka, it is what it is. But it ain't gonna be easy my, G. I got more lives than a cat."

I shook my head listening to my fearless soldier. "You good, B, Brad holding you down." I stared at the young boy. "So, just chill." I returned my focus on Goon. "Listen to me, you need to rest cause when we strike, you gotta be able to go all the way in, son," I drilled it to him uncut.

"Goon!" she yelled, I remembered her voice before she even entered the room. Our eyes locked the moment she was in the room. "Sorry, I didn't know you had company," she professed with a little boy in her arms.

I stood to my feet.

"I hear you, Rocket." Finally, that little nigga gave in, but I knew he didn't want to. I was just like him when those suckas tried to take me out, but thanks to Jae and Trap, I got my rest.

"You'll thank me later." I dapped that nigga up.

"You don't have to leave," said E'mon.

But I had to, Jae's words were playing over and over in my head. *"I'll kill you!"*

"You straight?" Trap questioned me before I could close the door to the whip.

"Yeah, I'm straight." I cut the engine on.

"Yeah, that's what you spittin' right now, but this the second time shorty came."

"It ain't that, my nigga," I cut him off not wanting to hear shit else 'bout ol' girl.

"It better be, cause I'd hate to bury you behind some pussy," he commented.

"Never! And that's on everything I love. I would never cheat on my wife."

****

We got to Kingsborough Projects in minutes. My heater was locked and loaded. "Yo', I'm at the door." I hit Scarface's line. *Click! Clack!* The door opened. "What's good?" I stepped past him as he held the door for Trap.

"I got it from here, B," I heard Trap telling the nigga.

The room was empty and clean, I couldn't even tell that Trap had murked a nigga here days ago. I took a seat at the table. Trap stayed standing, his hoodie was pulled all the way down over his face and his right hand was buried under his shirt. My muthafuckin' hitta. Scarface reached under the table and pulled out a black duffle bag.

"Fifty bands." He tossed the bag on the table. "And twenty more for the trouble," his words were said with an ill-feeling.

I eyeballed the nigga for a second before I said a word, "Twenty for my trouble." I tapped my chest. "That ain't what you owe me, son." I stood to my feet with my eyes locked in on that nigga, as I grabbed the bag. "All you owe me is fifty and that's all I'm here to collect." I unzipped the bag pulling the stacks out. I never want a nigga to say he gave me shit. I dropped the twenty bands on the table and zipped the bag back up. "Be careful, son." I walked past the nigga still standing. My words came from deep within.

Jamaica

Chapter 24

~Trap~

It didn't matter how much muthafuckin' love you showed a nigga. Or how many chances you handed out, there was always a nigga trying ya hand to see if they could win one over on you. Rocket had always been a standup nigga from day one. When his brother Ro tried to set him up, he still showed that nigga love turning the other cheek and striking when the time was perfect.

"You gotta keep niggas real close in this game, bruh," he would spit to me. "But when you do catch them slippin' you make sure you empty that muthafuckin' clip!" He stayed preaching to me. "I let a lot of shit slide cause you must think before you act. One simple fuck up can destroy you and everything you've worked hard for." Whenever he spat them jewels, I would soak his thoughts up like a sponge. I knew Rocket wasn't going to allow Scarface to do too much more. Son was on a time scale and didn't even know it.

"Gotta replace that nigga and rebuild another crew up, fam." I leaned my seat back but was still capable of seeing the streets due to the outside mirror as I listened to Rocket's plan.

"What you think, bruh?" he asked me. It didn't matter that he was the HNIC; he still valued my opinion as his right-hand man and brother. There was nothing but love and loyalty between us.

"I feel you. But who are you gonna send that way?"

"We'll figure it out, but for right now, I can't afford to clap that fool. Too much beef ain't never good for business. The murder rate will definitely rise to the roof I am sure that nigga got niggas that is willing to ride for him." He rubbed his temple. "Gotta be one step ahead in the game, fam."

"That nigga on second base, bruh," I referred to Scarface. "One more fuck up and I'ma tag them toes. Fuck the murda rate!"

'*Loyalty got royalty inside my DNA, Cocaine quarter piece. Got war and peace inside my DNA. I got power, poison, and joy inside my DNA...*' Kendrick Lamar's *DNA* played on Rocket's phone.

"What's happening, OG?" he greeted the caller with his foot still on the gas. "You already know pops." He turned his head in my direction for a split second. "Just me and Trap as always," he continued with his conversation.

I dug my phone out of my pocket, tapping on Pound Cake's info, and shot her a text.

//: *Get on a plane and let me know when you at my mom's spot. ~ Trap~*

After a few seconds, I got a response from her.

//: *Okay. ~Pound Cake~*

I eased my phone back into my pocket and returned my attention to the streets of Brooklyn with my gat in hand.

Chapter 25
~Rocket~

I had mad moves to handle, two out of state niggas that I supplied on a regular was in town for a re-up. "Call Ma Dukes and tell her to come outside." I tapped Trap's leg. "That's what's up, but you know me already. I don't tolerate bullshit," I was still on the call with my pops.
"Draymond," Ole' man called me by my first name.
"I'm listening."
"You need to put all moves on hold and handle that Country fuckin' problem," the base in his voice bossed the fuck up. "You must destroy that bridge before you move or that bitch gonna burn you."
I knew I had to find Cuba, fast. Everything OX was spitting was the truth. Ole' man had mad knowledge about the game. I had to crush Cuba in order for me to concentrate in the streets how I was supposed to. "One time is a problem, especially a big one. And it doesn't matter how many eyes you have, youngsta. Once you destroy the biggest problem, the little ones won't even matter." He coughed. "And that muthafucka is the biggest!" I was glad he was in my life now. "And if you gotta fuck the whole muthafuckin' New York for that bitch to show up, do it!"
"Already!"
"How are my grandkids doing?" He switched the conversation and his tone. I ran the fucked-up shit that Ashanti had done down to him. "Some bitches don't need to be breathing." I could feel his wrath through his words and I knew if he was free, he would have capped that bitch that birthed me, himself.

"It's all about timing, OG," I was so glad he had a phone on the inside. It allowed us to talk freely. "But onto a better note—" I paused. "You're going to be a grandfather, again." There was silence, but I could hear him breathing. "And it's a boy." My girls were my world, but having a little nigga gave me a different feeling.

"Congrats," he finally said breaking the silence. "You're a great father now," his voice cracked. "But there is nothing like a father raising his son." My pops had been gone since I was a child, taken away by a snitch made bitch nigga. But even though he missed out on a lot of things, he made sure I was okay no matter what.

"Shit, you doing it now," I voiced, meaning every word I said. "You still that nigga ole man and very soon muthafuckas gonna see that shit!" I was at Miss Judith's house. I watched her as she strolled to the passenger side with a smile on her face. Trap got the duffle bag from the back seat. "Hold on." I handed my phone over to her the second the window went down. She gave me this crazy look with her brows arched together. "Hello!" Then her beautiful smile appeared. I don't know what my pop was spitting, but I was happy to see her smiling.

A minute or so passed before she said anything, "I'll be waiting." She ended the call.

Trap gave her the bag as she passed me back my phone. "How are you doing, mom?"

"I'm doing well as long as my family is good," she responded looking at the both of us. She loves me like I was hers from the womb. No matter what we did, she was there riding, ten toes down.

Trap updated her about Pound Cake and Trap Jr.'s arrival before we pulled off. "Keep them eyes wide open out there in the jungle!" she said walking away from us.

I was a lucky ass nigga to have her in my life and as family.

****

"After these moves right here, bruh." I pulled into our main trap house to collect the work for the out of town niggas. "We're on a mission to take Cuba out."

"We can do that and still make bread, B," I schooled Trap the same way my OG schooled me earlier. "I can't afford to lose none of my soldiers by that nigga's hand, fam. So, we gonna find that bitch and end that chapter."

We gathered up all the work that was needed for the moves. Ten birds, fifteen pounds of that Hydro, a pound of pills for one nigga. Twenty live birds alone for the next nigga. l showed mad love to niggas in this game, but with my Brooklyn niggas, it was cheaper. Out of town niggas had to come out of their pockets, hard. Trick, the VA nigga had been traveling up here to see me since I got in the game to cop work from me. Playboy was always 'bout his bread, so in all, everything was gravy for both of us.

"You at the spot, B?" I hit his line.

"Posted up, cuz," he used his deep, down South accent.

"Bet that." I dropped the call, I was already at the location checking the scenery out. I had to stay one step ahead out in this bitch.

"Let's ride, Bruh." Trap had the Johnson book bag strapped on his back as he exited the car. I pulled my fitted down over my eyes as I departed from the whip. Flatbush Ave was always crowded, it didn't matter what day of the week it was, as long as the stores are open, people are on the move.

Tick is a short, stocky, look-alike *Kevin Hart* muthafucka. Every time I do business with partna, he's always fresh to death. "What's happening, cuz?" he greeted me in front of the store showing me all his thirty-two's like I'm a dentist.

"Trying to live like you," I boost his ego, scanning the area.

"Hard work my nigga, can get you like this," he bragged stepping back displaying his outfit.

Trap was across the street handling the exchange as we rapped about the next meeting. "Alright, fam," I said spotting Trap walking back to our ride with a shopping bag. "Next time, make that double."

"Say less."

We dropped that bag off to Ma's crib, too. "Make sure that's eight hundred thousand, mom."

"And then what?" Miss Judith was that down ass mother that we had. "We'll figure it out." We pulled off as soon as she got inside the house.

****

"You at the location, son?"

"Yeah, my nigga," his tone hit another level. "Been here for a hot minute now," he snapped like he the muthafuckin' plug.

I pulled the phone away from my ear. This niggas way outta line hard body. I chunked the call without saying another word. "Fuck that, I don't need that bread." I switched lanes to take me back to the trap spot.

"What happened, yo'?" Trap asked sitting up with the products at his feet noticing what I had done and said.

"Bitch ass nigga talkin' 'bout he's been there for a hot minute." I switched lanes again only to spot a fuckin' pig two cars behind us. "Cock succas two cars back." I leaned my neck to the side, keeping my eyes on the road and the cop. "Ain't no biggie."

Trap cocked a bullet in the chamber. The car in front of the pigs turned left. "Fuck them hoes," he rapped pure hate.

I'd be damn if I go back to jail for some fuck shit and not smoke me a cop. "I'ma switch lanes again, and if this cracker does too, you already know what the deal is." I was so glad Jae and the girls were at home.

"Say no more, bruh!"

Jamaica

Chapter 26

~Jae~

"'Bout bloodclot time yuh return mi phone calls," I answered the call watching the girls riding their bikes in the back yard. "Hello," I snapped. I pulled the phone away from my ear to make sure the call was still connected. "Chessan!" I barked but she didn't answer, instead, I heard a faint cry on the other end. "Bloodclot talk tu mi yo!" Even though I was big mad at her for telling our father my business, I pushed that shit off hearing her crying. "Sis, please talk to me," I begged.

"He found out about, Trap," she finally said and I felt relief. I thought some mega shit had happened.

"Who?" I had to get my heartbeat right.

"My boyfriend," she cleared her throat.

A *boyfriend*, I thought she was single with the way she was handling Trap when she was here.

"Ya boyfriend?" I asked to make sure I had heard her correctly.

"Yes, we been together for three years now."

This was the first time I was hearing about this nigga. "You couldn't have been in no relationship cause you was down here fucking this nigga," I got straight to the point.

"Sis, stop it."

"Stop spitting the truth?" I asked but never gave her enough time to answer. "Never! You made ya bed so now you gotta lay in that bitch." I needed to smoke me a fat blunt in order to tolerate shit like this.

Now I knew why she was so confused when I told her I was going to be holding Rocket down whenever he got his time.

Jamaica

"You put ya sexual life on hold, altogether?" she asked me.

"You damn right, three years ain't shit. Plus, I have other shit on my mind besides some nigga's funky-ass dick."

"Jae!" she screamed bringing me back from our conversation years ago.

"What?" I snapped. "What you want me to say?"

"He put his hands on me," she was crying.

"You fucked another nigga, Chessan! How the fuck you think he's supposed to react?"

"Really?" she whined.

I didn't care, right was right and wrong was wrong. "Yeah, really, cause if you was my bitch, I'd smoke ya ass. Fuck putting my hands on you and wasting my energy." *'What's the fucking point of being in a relationship if you're going to cheat?'* I thought.

"Fuck you!" she screamed ending the call.

I thanked God I was raised by my grandparents, they showered and showed love and loyalty to each other. So, I'll live by their actions and their words of honor till my last breath. I rubbed my stomach as I continued to watch my girls play with each other. Fuck Chessan, if she didn't like my comment, she knew where to find me. "Pussyclath sketall."

****

~Trap~

A nigga was already on the fucking run, so my stay free alert sensor was on high. I'll die before I let twelve muthafuckin' crackers and a judge seal my faith. Fuck outta here. That jail shit wasn't for a nigga like me.

"If that muthafucka hit those lights, fam, I'm squeezing!" I meant what I said.

"It is what it is, Trap." Rocket was down to ride no matter what.

I knew if I pulled the trigger that nigga would he finger fucking his, too. No questions asked. My feet bounced up and down nonstop as my eyes bore through the window at the outside mirror.

"Fam, just breathe easy." Rocket appeared unfazed by the situation at hand. He was calm as ever. "We can't react before this muthafucka, B," his voice was mad low.

I was hearing what he was saying but I was feeling something way different. *Fuck this pig*! "Fuck!" I snapped seeing the red and blue lights flashing behind us.

Rocket gripped his burner easing the vehicle to the side of the road. "Let's ride!"

I eased up in the seat, twisting my upper body around in the seat. Pussy ass cracker 'bout to stain the streets of Brooklyn.

Jamaica

Chapter 27

~Rocket~

As I maneuver the cat over to the curb, I clutch my heater, tighter. "Bruh, fuck that shit! Let's blaze it out with this muthafucka." Trap's expression had anger all in it, but I ignore his statement totally.

I pulled over, but instead of the cop car stopping it sped right past us with sirens blaring. "Shit!" I exclaimed feeling relieved. Trap had his burner aimed at the windshield. "Bruh, put that shit down." He didn't move or say a word. Bruh was in a daze. I had to reach over and lower the hammer. "Fam, what the fuck?" I was still in shock at the shit that had just gone down.

"That's the same shit I've been saying, Bruh," he finally spoke up. "God must have been on that cracker's shoulder whispering in his ear."

"Had to be," I agreed.

My phone had yet to stop vibrating. It was that bitch ass nigga, Quavo, from Jersey blowing my line the fuck up.

Nigga should have checked his tone temperature before he got out of line about me running late. I hit ignore as I pulled back out into traffic with the trap spot at the top of my list. "Let's drop this shit back off, son."

"Yes, indeed."

Twenty minutes after I dropped the work off, Quavo was still blowing my phone up. Back to back calls from ole boy were getting on my last nerves. "Speak," I answered.

"Ayo, it wasn't like that at all," he explained his tone was way different from earlier. "I need that shit," he pleaded, but I was paying way more attention to all the noise in the background that I was hearing.

Jamaica

"Get that nigga here!" I heard a voice demanding and it stood out.

"A'ight, where you at?" My instinct told me to see what this fuck nigga was up to. I hit the speaker button so Trap could hear what I was listening to.

"The same spot," he answered. "On Fulton Street."

I tapped my left ear and twisted my finger telling Trap by sign language to listen to the background. His brows arched as we looked at each other. "Alright meet me at Prospect Park, now." I dropped the call.

I was close by so that gave me enough time to switch up cars and grab an extra burner from Beam since I was just around the block from his spot. Fam came through for me without any questions.

"I'm telling you that shit sounds offbeat, son," Trap said as we were cooped up in the Nissan with a few extra pistols on deck.

We parked at the entrance between two black Jeeps, capable of seeing everyone that entered the park. Our seats were leaned back as we camped out, patiently. The sun beamed but the AC inside kept us right.

"You see that shit?" Trap asked me the second a black Denali entered the park with an Impala in tow.

"You know I did." I couldn't see inside either ride due to the tinted windows. "Another muthafuckin' Denali, bruh," Trap announced.

That nigga Quavo always came through in a simple ride, a Camry especially. One Denali had already pulled in right along the Impala.

"This shit is crazy," I spoke keeping my eyes on the entrance and the rides. "Fuck yeah." I hit Quavo's line but dude didn't answer. "Quavo, should've been here already."

"Nae, muthafucka came out them bitches, bruh," Trap informed me.

Seconds later my phone rang, it was Quavo. "Yo."

"I'm here, Bossman."

I hit him with, "A'ight, I'm 'bout to pull up. What you driving again?

"The same ride, my Camry."

Just like I thought. "A'ight, one son." I turned my cell phone off right after our conversation. "Nigga said he's already here," I vibed to Trap. "In his Camry, too, but ain't nae muthafuckin Camry pulled in." I was already heated at how that fuck nigga tried to carry me. Fuck that, that nigga was trying to cap me, had to be with how he was handling things. I hit Jae's line from my other joint. "What you doing, Island Gal?"

"Nothing."

"Keep them monitors on you hear me?"

"Say no more." She dropped the call.

Lil' momma was my rider, my down ass bitch, my wife. I didn't have to say shit else. She knew the lifestyle we lived, and she was down to ride for our family at any cost.

****

~Trap~

The parking lot was packed with cars. "Fam, this shit don't look like what you want to see, yo."

"I know right." We sat still for about fifteen minutes before anything moved.

The back doors of the last Denali opened. "Cuba?" Rocket's voice clapped in my ear.

Jamaica

"What the fuck?" I sat up watching the fuckery unfolded in front of us. Quavo stepped out of the Impala and walked directly over to Cuba. These niggas knew each other. "Pussy ass niggas!" My hand itched with fire from the heat of my burner.

"Niggas plotting on my demise, bruh." Cuba wanted Rocket gone since he wouldn't fuck with him no more since he'd been home.

Rocket's pops OX was right, we had to smoke this mufucka Cuba fast before he had us all flatlined. Cuba's bread was that long, he had access to niggas that we were in business with. Money ruled over loyalty with those niggas, but with us on this end. It was loyalty over everything, even family.

"Fuck that!" I pulled my hoodie over my head as I grabbed the handle of the door.

"Naw fam." He shook his head, pulling me back with his hand. This nigga stayed fucking with my gangsta vibe. "Way too many eyes and cameras, bruh." He kept his focus on the clowns.

"How the fuck you gonna let this shit slide fam and not address the problem?" Hate pumped through my veins.

"There's a time for everything, B. A time for everything," his voice was inaudible, but it thumped like four fifteens in a closed trunk.

I let the handle of the door go. From where we were I couldn't hear the conversation but from body language, Quavo was explaining to Cuba how Rocket had turned his jack off.

"I got a better idea, yo," Rocket said reaching into the console grabbing a pen and paper.

Chapter 28
~Jae~

When Rocket hit me from his other phone talking 'bout I needed to watch the monitors, I knew somewhere something was going down. So, I didn't request any information, I did what I was told to do. I ushered the girls into the house, as I double-checked my pistol to make sure nothing would hinder me from blasting a pussy hole straight to hell if they had the heart to run up in this bitch.

"Take a shower and get ready for dinner," I advised the little ones as I turned on all the cameras around the crib.

My mind raced like a horse on a racetrack. *What the fuck was going on? Where the hell was Rocket? How bad was the bloodclath problem he was facing?* I wanted to ring his phone, but I needed him to concentrate on the sight at hand, I needed him focused and alert.

"Lord, protect my husband and my brother." I closed my eyes. "Keep them safe from their enemies in your name I pray. Amen!" My grandmother always drilled in me to pray. "Pray and leave it at God's feet, Jae. He will do the rest." I opened my eyes gripping the gat under my shin as I stared the monitors down wishing a muthafucka would think stupid to try us especially when I had the .40 on my waist and not on safety.

****

~Rocket~

We sat for about thirty minutes before them muthafuckas got the picture. I was not showing up, I was a step ahead. One by one they pulled out of the parking lot never noticing me and Trap. "Pussy as niggas!" What they had in mind for me was a waste but what I had on my mental for them bitch ass niggas was incomparable. I waited a few minutes before I pulled out. "I'ma drop this joint back off and pick the ride up."

Within an hour we were pulling up at the crib. Jae and my girls greeted me at the front door. "Daddy!" They both screamed at the top of their lungs.

Jae leaned back against the front door pinning her hair up into a messy ponytail. I picked MiMi up and kissed her cheeks. "I missed you, beautiful," I spoke into her ear.

"I missed you way more, daddy." She stretched her little arms apart. It melted a G's heart. Moo on the other hand just smiled up at me as I ran my hand threw her braids. In them cold streets, I'ma beast, but with these girls, I'm all butter. I melt away around them.

"What's up sexy?" I admired Jae's sexy ass stand with her left hand on her hips, pushing her plumped ass all out.

"You know, locked and loaded," she replied and that shit turned me the fuck on.

"My gangsta bitch, I already know." I leaned in to sample her lips. "Damn."

"Ewww!" MiMi voiced in my arms and ears.

"Yes, ewww y'all," Moo added.

It caused all of us to laugh I let Jae know what was going down once dinner was over with and the girls were tucked away in bed.

"I want to be with you out there, Draymond."

I sighed rubbing my face with both hands. "You can't, baby." I looked up at her.

"Why?"

"Are you serious?" I asked her, knowing damn well she knew why. "You're carrying our seed and I'd be stupid if I let you out of my sight much less out in them streets. And you have to be here for the girls." I stood to my feet.

"Rocket, I can't afford to lose you." Her eyes blinked and before I could say another word, tears were streaming down her face. "I can't lose you!"

"You are not going to lose me." I held her in my arms as I took in her scent of strawberries. "Baby you are not going to lose me, I promise."

"On everything?"

"On everything, Jae. On everything that I love."

I made that ass tap out with some good muthafuckin' loving. Had her ass crying from her soul with my tongue before I closed my eyes. I hit Gotti's line at about three am when I woke up.

"Youngin' you straight?" he answered on the second ring.

"Hell yeah, I'm straight, but I need some help."

"Run it down to me, son."

I watched the monitors in the kitchen as I grabbed the paper from earlier that I had stashed away and read the information off to him.

"That's all you need?"

"That's all I need, Sir."

"Give me a few days or less and you can come by and pick it up. I'll let you know when it's done."

"Bet that." We chopped it up a little longer before I ended the call and headed back to the sheets with my wife.

Jamaica

Chapter 29

~Trap~

"Hello," I answered my phone, without even looking to see who was calling. Only a few people had my number.
"What?"
"What time is it?" I tossed the cover over my head. The blunt and liquor from last night knocked me on my ass.
"Nine a.m."
"What?" I pulled the phone from my ear to make sure the time was right. It was.
"Where you at?" I listened to Pound Cake's voice.
"Alright, tell mom to come get me from the basement."
That was our code for her to know that I was at Rocket's spot. "The basement?"
"Do what I say yo'?" I barked at her ass.
"Whatever!" she snapped banging the call in my eardrum.
Rude ass bitch,' I thought. "Fuck!" I stretched before I sat up in the bed. I had smoked three Bob Marley's by myself with a 1/2 a bottle of Henny. My head was spinning even though the room was pitch black.
I dropped back onto the bed reaching my arm out to grab the remote from the nightstand. I powered the flat screen while hiding my eyes from the light.
"Damn!" I expressed wishing I didn't have to get the fuck up.
I staggered to the bathroom at full speed ready to drain my manhood. The Henny had my bladder ready to explode. I pissed for what seems like an hour nonstop. I flushed the commode, washed my hands and brushed my teeth. I changed my Black Tee to a fresh white one, as I kept the jeans on from last night. I knew my mom would be on her way as soon as

Jamaica

she got the message from PoundCake to pick me up, and I didn't want to keep her waiting, or wake Rocket and the family up.

Ten minutes later, my phone was vibrating away. "Hello," I answered as I picked the Henny bottle up off the floor.

"Boy, I'm outside," my mom said ending the call without me answering. She hated when she had to wait on someone.

I eased out of Rocket's spot without waking anyone up. "Morning mom," I greeted my old lady as I stepped in her car.

"Morning," she mumbled.

I had to laugh cause she was never a morning person, but whenever her kids wanted her, she was there. No time or location could stop her from racing to us.

"You want to stop and get something to eat?" I asked as she was driving.

"No."

"I guess you'll make me something to eat then?" That brought a smile to her face.

We were her world, no matter how grown we were. We will always be her baby boys. Damn, I missed my twin. I knew she missed him more, so I eased the pistol out from my waist and placed it on my thigh. She had lost one, she had two left and I wanted to keep it that way as I stared out the mirror at the streets of Brooklyn.

Fifteen minutes later, mom pulled up at her spot. I addressed my son the moment I opened the front door and saw him in front of the television. "What's up, Little Man?"

"Nothing," he kept his gaze on the television. My nigga was growing up mega fast. The older he got the more he started to resemble his mother.

Damn, I missed my baby mother. "How are you doing?" I asked him as he played the game.

"Good." I sat across from him.

His focus was on the game. My mom went straight to the kitchen as I stared my youngsta down. He looked just like Tara especially when he smiled. He had her dimples, her nose, and smile. "

"You gonna always remember me, Trap." I took at moment to reminisce about Tara.

"Shit you act like you leaving a nigga or something?" We were booed up in our apartment.

"I'm just saying, silly." She kissed me. *"I'ma be right here with you."* She tapped my chest as she straddled me. *"Always in ya heart, Papi."* That she will always be, in my heart but our child together was a constant reminder of our love.

I got up and stepped toward my bedroom trying everything to not think about Tara. Pound Cake's sculpture under the sheets stood out, especially her ass. It was like two over-sized watermelons with a small waist to go along with it.

"I know you ain't sleep?" I stood by the closed door, taking in the sight. Damn, shawdy had it going on still.

"How can I when I haven't seen you in a hot minute?" She opened her eyes and I licked my lips. "How can I, Trap?" She flung the sheets off her exposing her body in just a bra and panties.

I grabbed my extra leg, kicked my Timbs off and pulled my shirt over my body. Fuck Chessan, that bitch hadn't answered my muthafuckin' phone calls, nothing.

"I missed you," she moaned sucking my neck as I spread her legs apart.

"I missed you." I attacked her body like a shark.

"I know you do." She bit my neck as I dug deeper and deeper inside her tunnel.

"Aaawww," she murmured taking all of me while trying to breathe. "Trap," she moaned my name over and over as I hit her walls like a racketball, back and forth I stroked. "Yaasss!" she sang as she threw the pussy back to me.

Sex with Pound Cake was that A-l pussy from the first time I got inside her panties, but this time, that shit was on a different level. It was super dumb wet. The kind you smoke a bitch for having.

"I love you," she professed staring into my eyes. I knew she meant what she was saying.

Instead of repeating the words, I flipped her over face down and ass up. I snatched her hair pulling her head back as I pushed her lower back in so I could arch that ass up. I needed her to feel every inch of me.

"Trap," she mumbled.

"Shhh!" I let her hair go hoping she would drop her head into the pillow to suffocate her loud moans. I gripped her ass checks so wide apart that her booty winked up at me. "Take this dick!" I said through clenched teeth, I felt her muscles as they squeezed my dick. She was at her peak. "Fuck!" I felt that shit in my toes, so I pulled out. "Aaarrrggghhh!" Then I bussed all over her ass hole.

"Really?" she said, I could hear the hurt in her voice.

I never bust off inside of her. I let my body fall beside hers, embracing her warmly. How could I turn her love down when she was nothing but loyal to me since day one? Even though she had another child before me, she always treated my seed like he was her own. Shorty was there for me when my twin got killed. She was my rock on the low. Late nights when I was crying my heart out, she was there. I'd fucked around and let Chessan into the picture not seeing the real precious stone that I had in front of me the whole damn time. Fuck, was I in love with two women and didn't know it? I let the thought roam.

"I don't want you to change who you are or what you stand for. All I am saying is this—" She took a long deep wind. "I've been with you and only you since Trap Jr. was two years old." I did the math, Jr. was almost eight, six years. She continued, "All I want is a title on us, Trap." Her tears hit my skin and they felt like blazing fire coals. "Nothing more, Trap," she voiced but her watered eyes said it all and more.

"I hear you shorty." She removed her body from my arms. "Where you going?" I quizzed her, but she didn't say anything.

I watched her body bounce as she pulled something from her luggage. "I've been in this shit with you far too long," she said with confidence. "I know about that Island bitch!" She snapped her neck in my direction. "I let that entire shit slide because I know how the game is—" she paused staring me down. "—more money, more bitches, and more drama!" She tossed the brown envelope in my direction.

It landed on the bed at my feet. I studied her reaction, but she demonstrated nothing as she got herself dressed. I kept my eyes glued on her, taking in her beauty. She was a redbone with a light glaze of honey, hips wider than a trailer, thicker than a double layer strawberry cake and even though she rocked weave, she had enough hair in that shit for two people. When I met Janell aka Pound Cake she was a stripper trying to make ends meet as a single mother and I admired her hustle and grind. Her son Lil' Man was two years older than Jr. Once I started fucking with her on a regular. I made her quit that gig to stay home and raise her son and help me out with Jr. She was the only woman besides my mother that Jr. knew.

"Don't let me be that bitch to send you outta here, Trap."

I let her words slide, for right now. When she left the room, I studied the envelope closely. It felt light as I popped the seal on it.

Jamaica

"What the fuck?" A picture of me and Chessan at the airport fell out and it had me sitting straight the fuck up. '*Where the fuck was Pound Cake at when this shit was going down,*' I wondered. I released the picture to see what else was inside. My nerves were already shattered seeing the flick of me and shorty. "What the fuck?" I breathed out in disbelief staring down at the item in my hand.

Chapter 30

~Rocket~

Days passed and everything was at a standstill. The trap houses in each projects that I supplied were jumping. But I informed each project manager to relax for a few days without any further explanation. Late nights up playing card and video games with my angels were priceless. Watching them grow up in front of me daily was a true blessing. I'm grateful that God allowed me to survive those bullets and deception to experience times like these. Having Jae in my corner and on my side was an extra blessing.

Trap had his seed and Pound Cake in town, so the time off was well needed for us all. Goon had healed up and was ready to start back running. Muthafuckin' days had vanished and still, I hadn't heard a word from Gotti, so I pulled my phone out and pressed a few buttons before placing it to my ear.

"What's up with you, youngin'?" he answered his end.

"Waiting on some good news from you," I shot right to the point.

"I'll be here, waiting." He ended the conversation.

It took me less than ten minutes to pull up at Gotti's spot. "Damn, did you drive or fly?" he questioned as he held the door with a chuckle.

"I had my foot on the mat, OG." I dapped him up, returning my answer with a smile stepping past him.

Our conversation went extraordinary well. He had everything I had asked for and more. "When you venture out, make sure you go correct." He handed over all the information I had requested on a white piece of paper. I shook my head listening to him even though I knew that already. "If you need assistance—" He took a sip from a cup that he had on the table in front of him. "I'm here," he continued. "And I have people that are willing to ride along, also."

One thing about me, I did my own work. But what I was about to tackle, I knew I had to go in real hard leaving everything at my feet. I let his words hang in the air for a second. Yes, I had my own team, but one more warrior I trusted wouldn't hurt.

"You should already know how I get down." I stood to my feet. "But let ya right hand know I will be hitting his line." I dapped him up, stuffing the information into my back pocket with a smile on my face.

****

"What's crackin' with you, son?" I was parked outside Goon's spot.

"You know, waitin' on some noise so I can shake, fam." Little nigga was always on his gunplay game.

Our eyes scanned the streets carefully from my ride. "Well, get strapped up. We rolling out tonight, B."

A smile appeared on his face instantly. He lived for days like this. "I'll be waitin'." He reached for the door.

"Just you though, let Brad stay around just in case we gotta hit his line from where we at."

"Say no more, B." He hopped out tucking the heater back under his shirt.

Bitch ass niggas tried to dismantle my empire and my life all in one, but they'd fucked all the way up. Tonight the little muthafuckas was gonna see bloodstains by a Shotta's hand and we was gonna dress the concrete the fuck up.

****

~Trap~

An EPT pregnancy test rested in my hands. "What the fuck?" The picture of me and Chessan didn't mean shit to what I was holding. "*Pregnant.*" I read the words out loud. I leaned my head back seeing the blunt facts in my hand. "How the fuck?" I questioned, but I knew that shit would eventually happen. I was hitting Pound Cake raw dog the majority of the time that we fucked. That was days ago when I got the news time from Pound Cake that she was having my seed.

"The only reason why I'm letting you go back to the A is to get Lil' man, and when you get back—" She smiled. *"I need you to start looking for a crib big enough for all of us."* I pulled her face up to mine. She didn't blink or look away, her eyes kept hold of mine, something I found extremely sexy in a woman. *"You gonna handle that other shit, or you want me to?"* I knew she was referring to Chessan, so I acted dumb.

"What other shit, shorty?"

"Handle it and do it fast." She knew what I needed to handle.

"Do your end, shorty." I kissed her forehead leaving the room to chill with my son.

I whooped Jr.'s ass bad in *Call of Duty*. Growing up me and Tray played basketball all the time, we had games, but mom made sure we weren't stuck to the T.V. either. That's how I met Rocket, on the basketball court, but people that didn't know thought we came from the same womb.

Ding! Dong! The doorbell had me on my feet. "To ya room." I touched Jr.'s shoulder.

"Daddy," he whined.

"Now!" My burner was never far from me.

Jamaica

My mom was already asleep so who the fuck could it be ringing her damn doorbell. She didn't have friends that I knew of. My phone beeped as I headed for the door.

"Fam, it's me." Rocket's name appeared across the screen.

I unlocked the door, but kept my pistol on my finger tip, just in case. "Damn, nigga, you could've called me, bruh." I closed the door behind him.

"Shit, don't tell me you scared, nigga?" he joked tossing me a bag of some orange and yellow looking weed.

"Never!"

"Good, cause we got mad shit to handle." He pulled a sheet of paper out of his pocket before taking a seat.

"Run it down, fam!" As I rolled the blunt up we exchanged information.

"What you gonna do with Jae's folk?"

"It's dead, my nigga. Dead!" I twisted the blunt up ready to spark that muthafucka until Pound Cake entered the room.

"Rocket, how are you doing?" she greeted my brother.

"Good and you?"

"I'm peace, can't complain," was her come back. "I'll let you men be," she said leaving us.

I couldn't help but stare at all that ass as she walked away.

"Handle ya business, fam. I'll be in the ride waiting." Rocket snatched the blunt out of my hand shaking his head. I talked to Pound Cake and my son before I left the crib. "Let me know when you leaving for the A."

"You know I will."

"Trap!" I was halfway out the door when she yelled my name.

"Yeah." I turned around to face her.

"Be safe."

"Always, shorty." I tapped my toolie. "Always!"

Chapter 31
~Jae~

Since I wasn't talking to Chessan at the moment, I hit my friend Ribbon up. Even though we didn't hang out, we had each other's backs since day one. I recalled our first encounter. *We were in the grocery store, and she was ahead of me in the cash outline.*

"Your total is one hundred, forty-five dollars and sixty cents," the clerk at the counter said.

Ribbon had all her groceries packed by the bagger as she dug into her purse for her money "Damn!" she yelled in frustration as she came up with nothing. The clerk was running out of patience as she blew bubbles from her gum. Ribbon reached in her pants pocket, but she didn't come up with a dime. "I'm sorry, I left my purse with my money at home," she said sounding and looking embarrassed.

The bagger started to unpack all the groceries into a shopping can at the side. "Here you go," I said reaching up and leaning over my cart to pay the bubble popper.

The clerk looked at me like I had ten heads, but I was taught to bless people at any time, and my time had come to do just that. Our relationship started there, and it was icing on the cake because she was also Jamaican. She returned the favor to me by allowing me to smoke and trash J-Money's body at her chop shop that she ran.

"Wah a gwaan, baby girl?" I hailed her up as soon as she answered her phone.

"Jae!" she screamed out with excitement. "What a gwaan with yuh mi big triend?"

Jamaica

Even though she had been in the states for more than fifteen years, her accent was still heavy and thick like she had just arrived in America.

"How are the girls doing?"

"Jae, they are growing up so fast," I could hear the joy in her voice. "But they miss their father so much," then there was sorrow.

Her girl's father, Rich got killed by some niggas that he was running within the streets, that shit destroyed her mentally. Here she was now raising two beautiful girls all by herself.

"I know they do, Rib." I used the name that I gave her. I don't know how Moo and MiMi would be if they didn't have Rocket around. "And I know you do, too, my sista. But you gotta stay strong," I encouraged her.

"I'm trying, Jae, but some days are just hard as ever," she stated. I didn't know how she was feeling not having Rich around at all, but I knew I was almost knocking at death's door when I thought Rocket wouldn't recover from them bullet wounds. "How are you doing?" She switched her spirit around.

"I'm good, making it do what it do." I smiled knowing what I was about to tell her would have her smiling. "I'm pregnant."

"Oh, my gossshhh!" she screamed at the top of her lungs. "How far along are you?"

"Almost six months and I'm ready to have this little boy."

"Oh, my God! You having a boy?" Excitement filled her voice.

"Yes, mi friend."

"Mi know Rocket happy as ever?" We switched back to our language.

We talked for about two hours about everything that was happening in our lives. Vibing with Rib had me in a great mood until she brought up the conversation about the cowards that took her true love away.

"Did you find out who was responsible for that fuck shit?"

I had told her a long time ago that I would handle the men that had taken Rich away, all she had to do was find out who was behind his murder and hand the news down to me. She had scratched my back and now it was my time to scratch hers.

"Yes, I found out who was responsible for it," she said after a long pause.

Her answer caught me off guard, I had to stop moving or I would've stumbled over my own feet. "Why didn't you call and tell me, Ribbon?" I went back to her name.

"It's not going to bring him back, Jae." I heard her sniffling.

"Shit, it won't," I was real. "But you'll be able to get some closure, though." I was hurting because my friend was in pain.

I knew avenging his death wouldn't bring him back but fuck that shit. Their mommas, wives, girlfriends, baby mothers, children, what the fuck ever was going to feel what she was feeling plus more fucking with me and my team.

"Who is it, Rib?" Silence, but I knew she wouldn't hang up on me. "Ribbon, who was behind that shit?"

Her response caused me to sit down instantly. "What?" I held onto the side of the sofa. "On my life and my unborn son. I can promise you that bloodclot pussy hole a guh pay. Mark mi words!" Tears streamed down my face from all the anger I had built up in me.

Jamaica

Chapter 32

~Rocket~

I didn't give a fuck if the President of Cuba was affiliated with Castro aka Cuba, his ass was gonna get touched by this Brooklyn Shotta. Muthafuckas lived by that pistol, so they or the ones they love are gonna die by that bitch. That was always my motto. Bitch made Quavo had teamed up with Cuba after I had been nothing but one thousand with that nigga. So, I had to pay homie a visit in New Jersey, first. I had written down the license plate number to each vehicle that day when Quavo was supposed to pick the workup, but instead, he had Cuba with him for the ride. '*How did they know each other?*' I pondered ever since seeing them together. Gotti had his people do some research for me, getting me all the addresses on deck.

"How ya vest?" Jae helped me strap it up.

Beside a great man, there is always a great woman holding him down. "Good." I smiled down at her feeling untouchable with her love, along with the vest. "I'm mad as fuck, though." She twisted her lips up at me. "Why baby?"

"I didn't get invited to the party." She pouted sullenly.

Lil' momma was hardheaded as fuck, but I damn sure wasn't going to let her have her way, this time. Fuck no! "Stay put and hold this bitch down." I glanced around our house before locking my eyes back on my Al.

"You ain't said nothin' partna," she expressed before tipping up on her toes to tonguing me down.

"Don't let me change my mind and stay in the crib, I preached to her after her lips left my mouth.

"Hell navy," she proclaimed. "Go show them niggas that Brooklyn breeds nothing but last of a dying breed, Shottas!"

Jamaica

****

"How you feeling, G?" I asked Goon as he packed his heaters up with bullets.

"Ready to ride, fam," he replied paying attention to his tools. "Ice?"

I had hit Gotti's right hand up and inquired if he was interested in taking a trip with me. All he asked was, "What kind of party is it going to be?"

"A send a nigga on his way party."

"Count me in." He didn't ask who, when, why or where.

As he sat in the driver seat of the *Acura* that Gotti had provided us with. I asked him was he straight. "I came out the pussy ready, gangsta," he replied in a gruff voice. "Both my parents were about that life," he said staring me dead in my eyes.

That's all I needed to hear. It was ten p.m. when we left Brooklyn. Trap lit a blunt as we hit the road in my favorite car, an Impala and we led the way for Ice and Goon.

****

Hours later, we were in Brick City of Jersey. We were camped in Quavo's neck of woods. "Seventeen-twenty is his location number, youngin'." Gotti let me know.

"*Seventeen-twenty*." A few houses up from where we had parked, Quavo had his mom, baby mama and daughter stashed away according to Gotti's source. '*How the fuck we getting in that bitch?*' My mind wondered as Trap pulled his ski mask over his face ready to start the party.

As I studied my surroundings, I realized this muthafucka was living real well. The houses were about a half a block apart from each other and big as fuck. Just as I was about to exit the car, an all-white 760 BMW swerved passed us almost taking the outside mirror off.

"What the fuck?" Trap voiced.

If I wasn't on a mission tonight I would've rained bullets all through that bitch. "Muthafucka's drunk bruh."

The car slowed up and stopped right in front of Quavo's spot. I looked over at Trap before I rest my eyes back in front of me. What's understood doesn't need to be explained. The brake lights disappeared, and the car pulled right up the ramp of 1720. That bitch Lady Luck was definitely on my side. We were already out the ride traveling mighty fast on our feet toward the spot. The car stopped but we didn't. Ice and Goon were right behind us. The passenger door opened, and I touched Trap's arm causing him to stop. We were all dressed in black from head to toe. So, getting noticed would be hella hard to do. The driver's door flew open and I heard someone gagging like they were about to throw the fuck up. I pointed to Trap to take the passenger side as I grabbed the other side.

"Pussy ass nigga!" I jammed the hammer to the side of the nigga's head and just like that liquid exit from his mouth all over the inside of the ride.

"Pussy you better not make a sound," I heard Trap telling the other person.

The nigga that released all the liquor over the car, wasn't Quavo. I'd never seen this clown before. Trap snatched the dude out and closed the door. I tried to pull ole boy out, but the pussy held onto the steering wheel.

Click! Clack!

I cocked one in the chamber, the nigga bitched up and eased his hands up. I stuffed the toolie right in his mouth, rattling a few teeth loose. Pain was written all over his face, he sobered up, instantly. His eyes displayed fear, as his hands tried to grip the burner. I swatted his hands sharply as Ice rested his pistol at his temple. "Pussy, don't try me!" I uttered. I was ready to leave him exactly where I met him.

Chapter 33

~Trap~

"Lead the way since you wanna lead niggas to us!" I was mad hype and ready to leave Quavo's bitch ass right in the car, slumped the fuck over, but I knew Rocket wanted answers.

"What the fuck?" Quavo tried to turn his body around but my heater kept his head straight. All the money this nigga had invested in a crib, his bitch ass didn't have any motion sensors around his crib or cameras. As we climbed the stairs, I prepared myself for the porch light to come on, but it never did. Not a smart dude at all.

"You better punch the right fucking code in, B," I let the fool know as we stood in front of the front door.

"Whatever you want, I can give up," he confessed, not realizing who the fuck we really were.

"Punch bitch." I jammed the hammer forward and forceful to the back of his head. "Now!" I said through clenched teeth. I moved my head to the side to see what he was typing in the digital pad, He pressed 8 and stopped. "Don't make me leave you right here!" I let the pussy know. 8-7-3-2. He punched in and his head dropped as I heard the door click open. "Push the door, B." He did as he was told.

The second the door opened completely the light came and brighten up the entire room. My eyes shifted around the room quickly to make sure we were alone and no one else was present at the moment.

"Kay!" he yelled, and I gun butted that nigga sending him forward.

I heard the door close behind me as Goon dashed past us with the pistol leading the way. "Another muthafuckin' word from you son and they gonna tag ya face to a T-shirt." He grabbed the back of his head with both hands.

I motioned with my pistol for his bitch ass to take a seat.

"Anything you want, I can provide," he insisted.

"Can you provide loyalty?" Rocket voiced as he pushed the driver beside Quavo on the sofa.

"*Loyalty?*" he mumbled with his eyes pierced on Rocket.

Rocket pulled his ski mask up exposing his face. "Yeah, nigga, *loyalty*! Can you provide that?"

Quavo looked like he was about to pass out when he realized it was Rocket. "Man—ayo—man," he stuttered trying to peace his words together. Ice returned with an older lady carrying a baby in her arms. From the looks of her hair, she was fast asleep. "Don't hurt her!" Quavo screamed trying to rush towards Ice but I sent his ass flying back to the sofa with a Mike Tyson bullet.

"How the fuck did I get caught up in this bitch?" the driver said. "Yo, B, let me bounce, yo!' he begged Rocket. "I don't even know this nigga." He pointed at Quavo.

"Like that?" I couldn't help but laugh out loud. Niggas didn't have any morals, principles or loyalty. If me and my nigga were in a situation like this, one thing for sure, we would be fighting for our lives together before we ever crossed over on each other.

****

~Rocket~

I pulled the silencer from my pocket attaching it to my toy. The driver's eyes studied my movements, but I didn't give a fuck. I was tired of hearing this nigga bitching. Ice sat the old lady with the baby across the room.

I heard him telling her, "Bitch, you better not say a fucking word, hoe."

"This shit is fucking crazy!" The driver expressed as tears streamed down his face. "Mane, I got a family, yo," he begged with his hands joined together like he was praying. "B, I'm telling you right now, if you let me go."

Tu! Tu! I cut his words off with two to the head. His eyes bulged as his body leaned all the way back. Quavo jumped up and I clapped him right in his shoulder. "Pussy ass nigga, lean back!"

"Arggghhhh!" he hollered out in pain as he applied pressure to his shoulder, blood-soaked the white fur sofa. "Anything you want, I can provide," he whined.

"Can you provide loyalty?" I asked again. "How the fuck you know, Cuba?" Before he could answer my question, Goon appeared in the room with a redbone.

As soon as she saw Quavo's face she took off toward him crying. "Arrrggghhh!" he yelled feeling the pain of being hit up.

"I ain't got all day, nigga!"

"Fuck you!" he responded.

I clapped back. *Tu! Tu!* I bullet fuck his bitch. Her body dropped at his feet she didn't even see it coming. "Get that baby, Ice."

The old lady didn't want to hand over the little girl but as soon as Ice placed the hammer to her head, she knew she had lost the fight.

"Alright! Alright, I'll talk!"

The nigga met Cuba while I was locked up, so they started doing business but once I came home, he stopped. Cuba's prices were mad high, plus the product wasn't like it used to be.

"That shit was fucking my clientele up," he whined. Cuba found out he was linking up with me.

"And?"

"He said." Quavo took a deep breath of wind. "He said that if I set you up he would give me a million cash."

I had to chuckle, I rubbed my temple. "A million dollars?" I knew Cuba wanted me six feet deep but I'd be damn if I let that pussy get me first.

"He knows you killed his mother and son," Quavo continued. "So, he reached back and touched your crew."

As soon as the word crew left his mouth, Goon's toolie spoke revenge on Quavo's mother's body. Her back hit the wall and before it could even slide down another bullet was at her head.

"No!" he screamed trying to get up, but I hit his left leg up. Tears ran from his eyes like a flood. Pussy muthafuckas cry when that bullet hit, but a real nigga will always have a smile on their face, not some tears. Time waits for no man and with that, I clapped that nigga to eternal sleep. Cuba's face flashed across my mind and I wished there was a way that I could reach out and touch that succa tonight, but I was at peace for the moment with Quavo silent.

"What you gonna do with that little bitch?" Goon asked referring to the baby. "Whatever you want, G."

Ice removed his hands from the little girl like he was dropping a bone to a clog. Before her body could hit the floor or before a scream could leave her mouth, Goon sent hot slugs her way with a smile on his face. Her little body ripped into pieces.

"My nigga kids ain't got a daddy, so fuck that bitch!" He kicked her dead body before we bounced from the scene.

Chapter 34

~Jae~

No matter how hard I tried to go to sleep, I just couldn't. I would doze off, but never for long. Rocket leaving Brooklyn had me scared to death but knowing that he had Trap, Ice and Goon with him gave me a little bit of peace. But I wouldn't be able to close my eyes completely until he was back in my arms.

"Fuck!" I stretched my arms out under my pillow, but I didn't feel what I was looking for. Fear gripped my soul, after that shit with Ashanti, I'll never get caught slipping without one with me. I picked the pillow up off the sofa spotting my banger in the crease. All kinds of thoughts ran through my head and I let them all slide, except one. Quickly, I dashed up from the sofa, tucking my burner under my shirt with a smile on my face. I checked in on the girls, they were fast asleep.

"Fuck!" I checked the time it was 2:17. "Not bad," I talked to myself.

I switched my clothes within seconds, putting everything back on. Within minutes I had the alarm set and pulling out the garage with one thing on my mental. Karma is sweeter than getting fuck by Rocket for hours. There's no way I was just going to sit back and let this shit slide. "Fuck no, arrgghhh!" A sharp pain hit me in my ribs causing me to use my left hand to rub my tummy.

The closer and closer I got to my destination, the more my son moved around in my belly. "Come on, D.J. chill." I was going to make my son a Junior for sure. The second I said his name, he stopped. "A momma's boy, already," I mumbled smiling.

Jamaica

Ashanti was still living in the same spot that she had whooped my ass at. I had driven up and down the block to see if anyone or anything looked suspicious. The dumb bitch didn't even reach out to Rocket to see if her daughter was breathing or not. Ashanti's actions alone expressed that she didn't give a fuck about MiMi at all. My blood bubbled all over just thinking about all she had put MiMi through.

"Pussyclath sketal!" The rage I had for her returned with the blink of an eye.

I parked my car at the end of the block, double-checked my appearance and hopped out. Only two streetlights were on, and they were all the way at the other end of the block. My black hoodie covered my head all the way up and the black eyeliner I used to alter my lace, helped. I stuffed my hands inside my hoodie and took off. This shit was fucking personal, way too personal for me to just let it go. The hoodie covered my stomach perfectly as my feet strutted towards her house. I took a big gulp of air from the breeze that flew my way.

How the fuck was I getting into her house this time of night without making any noise or disturbing the neighborhood? Woman to woman, I had to show this bitch that a child was a gift that should be cherished and loved. From a real bitch to a bum bitch I had to let her understand that I was a gangsta, a straight bloodclath Shotta. A dimmed light from her living room was visible through her blinds that were half open. It was now or never for me to make my fucking move.

Tap! Tap! I knocked before I turned my back to the door with my head ahead of me as I listened closely to any sounds that I could hear. A minute passed and nothing happened. I knew this bitch was home, her car was in the driveway. Just as I was about to knock again, I heard the unthinkable. *Click! Clack*! Whoever was opening the door, didn't even ask who

Blood Stains of a Shotta 3

was knocking. The moment I saw the knob turning, I prepared myself.

"Why the fuck you left your keys?" Ashanti's stupid ass voice rang before she saw my face.

The whiff of liquor reefed from her words before I even laid my eyes on her. The instant I saw my window of opportunity, I took it. *Bam*! I clocked her with the butt of the gun sending her flying backward.

"Aaahhh," she said hitting the floor.

She had lost her balance, I kicked the door shut with the back of my sneakers. I knew I needed to make this mission real quick before whoever she was waiting on returned. I pulled my hoodie from over my head. I needed her to see my face.

"Not you again," she pronounced.

This time, I didn't need to communicate, she saw and knew my face and that's all I craved, *Boom! Boom*!

Jamaica

Chapter 35

~Rocket~

Jae was fast asleep when I got inside our bedroom. Usually, she would've been up waiting on me with her hammer at her side.

"Bae," I whispered stripping the clothes off me, but she didn't answer. "Jae," I whispered a second time as I rubbed her thigh causing her to stir.

"Yes?" She rolled over to face me.

"I'm back, bae, everything went good." She sat up rubbing her eyes. "I'ma hit the shower. Can you handle them clothes for me?"

"That's not even a question you should ask. You already know I got you."

The hot water eased my body but damn sure not my mind. The little girl's body and Goon's bullets replayed in my head the entire way home. When you played with a nigga's heart and soul everything the enemy loved was in danger. My heart was twice that and more in order to protect my family and those that I love. After about twenty minutes, I grabbed the towel to dry myself down. Jae was wide awake watching cartoons on the T.V. when I climbed in the bed with her. She pushed her warm body up under me as I inhaled her vanilla scent.

"Got Quavo's whole family tonight." I was glad to be finally home with my family.

"I can't wait till you get, Cuba," her vocal sound spat venom. "I am glad you wiped the whole family out."

"Baby mama, mom, and a nigga that was there—" I paused remembering how Ice dropped the little girl's body from his hands. "—even his newborn daughter."

"Good!" I felt her lips curve up against my skin. "Pussyclath dem wanted yuh dead!" The pain in her voice as she spoke had her mad. "Fuck them dead muthafuckas!" She touched my manhood. "Can you put me to sleep?"

****

~Jae~

I hadn't been to sleep since I got back from handling Ashanti. I was pretending to be knocked out the whole time Rocket was trying to wake me up. He would be mad as fuck if he knew I had left his babies in the house by themselves, to hit the streets up while I was six months pregnant with our son. Especially, to do a hit.
"Yuh ready feh meh feh put des pum pum pan yuh?"
"You know I stay ready for that pussy," he replied. "Mmmhhhh," he moaned as I unleashed the beast. I began stroking his extra leg, raising it from the grave. "Ahhhhh, yasssss baby," I purred as I watched my dick rock up biting my lips. I couldn't wait to swallow my man the fuck up.

****

~Rocket~

When Jae started talking that Patwha, my dick had no choice but to salute her voice and stand the fuck up. She slowly placed all my dick in her mouth. I could feel her tonsils as she started deepthroating me, she didn't even gag. She was making it nice and sloppy.
"Mmm," she moaned as she was sucking my dick.

The vibration of her humming had a nigga ready to tap the fuck out. "Fuck!" Jae was my freak. "Suck that shit, baby." I held onto her hair from the root.

As I felt the need to shoot my seed down her throat, I made her stop. "Succa!" She shined smiling. Her head game was that damn good.

"Bend that ass over!" I told her.

As she got on all fours, I watched her fat pussy from the back. I spat on her asshole and watched as it slid down to her pussy. I slurped her up and had her screaming.

"Oooo, baby." That pushed a nigga to go harder. Lil' momma was trying to pull away from me but I gripped that ass firmly. "Baby, meh 'bout feh cum," she sang the language that drove me fucking crazy.

Her body jerked and I knew her juices were about to be all over my face. It didn't even take ten seconds for her to release her vitamins.

"Damn you tryna drown a nigga?" I clowned as I laid her on her back. I watched as she got her breathing under control. "I love you!" I let her know. "Uhhhhh, I love you!" I slid up into her already wet pussy slowly.

"I love you too, Rocket!" she continued.

"Mmm!" I gave her what she wanted, long, deep strokes as I took my time not trying to put a dent on my son's head.

"Rocket!" She pulled me down to her face.

"Yes," I said.

"From my soul, I love you!"

"Come sit on this dick," I said as we flipped over.

Jae rode a nigga like a horseback rider, up, down. As she held onto my chest. "Damn, Ma!" I licked her breasts as I watched her ride me. "I'm cummin' again, Rocket!"

"Cum on daddy's dick, baby." I gripped her ass cheeks spreading them apart so I could get all the way up in her.

Jamaica

"Baby, fuck me harder," she moaned out as her head hit my chest.

That sent a nigga off the edge as she matched my rhythm. Together, we held on to each other as our hearts raced at the same speed.

Chapter 36

~Trap~

"What you doing?" I asked Pound Cake the second she answered my call.

"You see what time it is, Trap?"

It didn't matter what time of the day it was where she was, she always answered my calls. "I know what time it is." I eased my body under the sheets wishing I had her next to me. "Go back to sleep, shorty."

"Love you," she said before I could drop the call.

I knew her heart had my name written all over it. "I know and keep it that way." My body was tired, but my mind wasn't.

After about twenty minutes my eyes still wasn't shut. I stared up at the ceiling wondering where I went wrong with Chessan. Visions of her invaded my thoughts, like the way she said my name when I was hitting it from the back. The way her body moved when she was in front of me. The way her scent lingered on me for days.

"Fuck!" I snatched up my phone hitting my contacts.

As the phone rang in my ears my heart stopped as I waited to hear her answer my call. After the sixth ring, her voicemail came one. *"You've reached Chessan, please leave a message and I'll get back to you as soon as I can."*

I ended the call and reached for the blunt that I had already twisted up. I took three good puffs of my medicine trying to ease my mind. The vibration of my phone caught me off guard this time of the morning, it was 5:17.

"Hello," I answered as the smoke escaped from my mouth.

"Who is this?" I pulled the phone from my ears to see if I was hearing right. Chessan's name was on my screen, but a nigga was in my ear. "Who is this?" he repeated.

Jamaica

"Where Chessan at?"

"Who are you?" he raised his voice waiting on me to respond.

"Fuck that bitch, homie, you can keep her!" I chucked the call in his ear hoping that bitch heard me loud and clear if she was around. No wonder shorty ain't been reaching out or answering my phone calls. She had a nigga this whole time. Had me all caught up in her web of lies and deceit. I erased her number and pics from my phone and memory as I puffed on some good ass ganja. Before the blunt was done, I didn't even remember laying down.

Chapter 37

~Rocket~

My fucking phone had been ringing on and off for about twenty minutes nonstop. I reached for Jae's body, but her spot in the bed was empty. "Fuck!" I snatched my phone up from the nightstand. "Hello?"

"Rocket, she is dead!" Miss Pam screamed, and it felt like flames. "My baby is dead!" she continued to wail.

My body froze as I listened to her cries. *Dead*, the word bounced over and over in my head. "How?" I finally had the courage to ask.

"Someone shot her, Draymond," her tone raised. "Someone shot my fucking child."

"Where are you?" I was in the closet trying to find something to put on, fast.

"I'm at Kings County!" she replied between sobs.

"I'm on my way!"

Cuba's face flashed in my mind. How the fuck did I sleep so hard on this clown?

"Baby!" Jae entered the room. "Are you up?"

"Ashanti is dead!"

She twisted the top off the bottle of water she was carrying and took a sip. "How?"

"Someone shot her." I laced my sneakers up.

"Well, damn!"

I let her slick comment go, this damn sure wasn't the time. Plus, I knew she didn't give a fuck about Ashanti at all. "I know right. How the fuck am I going to tell, MiMi?"

"I don't know." She took a seat beside me, taking another sip of the water.

Jamaica

"You are going to help me do it." I held her hand as I looked into her eyes. But she dropped her head. "If you want me to." Then she lifted her head up slowly.

"I am." I washed my face and brushed my teeth before I checked in on my girls, then kissed them on their foreheads before leaving their rooms.

"Where you going?" Jae questioned as I reached for the front door.

"To the hospital."

"Hospital, fuck for what?" Lines formed in her forehead.

"To see, Miss Pam and Ashanti's body."

"The bitch is dead and you running to see her?"

"Jae."

"Jae, my muthafuckin' ass, nigga! What the fuck I look like, Rocket?"

I really wasn't in the mood for Jae's slick ass comments. "Drop that shit, baby."

"Fuck you telling me to drop some shit when all that bitch did was give you fucking pure hell!"

"Jae!"

"The bitch is dead and you running to see her one last time," she snarled. "You still fucking that dumb bitch!" she barked slugs at me.

Before I knew what was happening, my hands was lifting her up off the floor. "Bruh, let her go!" Trap was peeling my fingers from around her neck.

Jae's tears ran down her face as she stared shots at my head. Finally, I let go as I backed toward the door.

"Are you, okay?" I heard Trap asking her.

"Fuck!" As I drove, guilt hit me. Cuba had touched home. Even though the bitch was dead, I wished he wasn't the one that did the job, but I knew better. "Fuck!" I punched the steering wheel. Jae's words cut real fucking deep and they caught me way off guard, causing me to take my frustration out on her.

"You have to kill that muthafucka, Rocket. Or he is gonna cause you trouble," OX's words clapped.

****

I found Miss Pam in the front lobby, crying. I embraced her as her body rocked back and forth in my arms. "My baby is dead!" she boohooed. "Dead Rocket, *dead*!"

I just held her until she calmed down a little. "Who found her?"

"Her boyfriend," she said getting herself together, as we took a seat. I waited patiently for her. "They were drinking, enjoying the night together," she said. Tears ran nonstop down her cheeks. Ashanti's nigga got a call so he told her he had to make a move but would be right back. Miss Pain kept going, "He left her in the bed only to return home finding her on the floor in their living room—" she paused. "—dead! He's cooperating with the police." She wiped her face. "He is not a suspect." I sat still and listened to her vent about Ashanti and all the stuff they had been through together. She said, "She loved you, Rocket."

"At one point she did, but something happened, and she changed up on me, Miss Pam."

"But you always held her heart." I let her talk not wanting to upset her. "How are we going to tell, MiMi?"

I switched up the convo. "I don't know, but we have to." I reached in my pocket and pulled out a knot. "If you need more, let me know." I handed her the money as Miss Pam's family arrived.

"Rocket!" She tried to push it back to me but I denied her. "It's the least l can do."

Jamaica

****

~Jae~

That shit Rocket pulled had me fucked all the way up. I knew I was supposed to tell him, but l knew if I had brought the convo up, he would've stopped me.

"You should have told him," my conscience sounded off not allowing me to sit still.

"Jae!" Trap called out my name. "What happened?" he questioned me.

"He got a fucking phone call stating that Ashanti was dead," I whispered as I paced the room not wanting to wake the girls up.

"What?"

"Yeah." I dropped my head feeling guilty for not telling Rocket the stunt that l had pulled.

"Did you do it?" he clapped back. I heard him, but I didn't answer, all I did was stare right through him. "I'ma wake the girls up." He stood to his feet. "And take them to my mom's."

I picked my head up and smiled. "Thank you," I said before I walked off. Fuck that dead bitch, Ashanti. Her ass should've loved MiMi and not had abused her. She was where she needed to be six bloodclot feet under."

Chapter 38

~Trap~

"Bruh, I'm at mom's spot with the girls. "I informed Rocket.

"Where is, Jae?" My nigga was down, it was all in his voice.

"I left her at the spot, fam." He was silent. "I heard about Ashanti."

"Cuba did this shit, bro."

I let his words fall, not responding to his statement. "Bruh, go home and fix that shit with Shotta," I advised, "She loves you."

"Trap, thank you."

"Man, you already know, it's death before dishonor." My mom was sitting on the porch with me as I sparked the blunt up. She knew what I did and didn't care, as long as I didn't do it around my seed. "Jae did that shit to Ashanti." I took a puff off the blunt.

"Why you say that?"

"Jae hated Ashanti from day one, because of how she carried Rocket. She only put up with her because she didn't want Ashanti to hold MiMi as a pawn and away from Rocket. But all that shit went out the window when Ashanti started mistreating MiMi." My mom stared out on the lawn as I put her up on game. "The last thing Ashanti did to MiMi broke Rocket all the way down." Ma looked over at me, so I kept going. "And one thing for certain, Jae don't like to see Rocket hurt behind the ones he loves."

"She loves him to the core, just like Pound Cake loves you," My mom rapped nothing but the truth.

No matter how hard I try to think otherwise, Pound Cake's love showed its true meaning, faithfully. "How about you and

Jamaica

the kids chill while I take Pound out for something to eat?" I shortened her name.

"Boy, you just want me to stay in the house and babysit." She chuckled as she got tip fanning the smoke away.

****

"Where you wanna go!" Pound asked me as she steered the Audi.

"As long as we are in Brooklyn, I'm good shorty." My toolie was resting on my leg at my fingertip as I stared out the window.

"You ever thought about leaving the streets?" she questioned with her eyes on the road.

"The streets is my home for, right now, but someday I plan on letting it all go."

We didn't say anything else for minutes until she broke the ice, "I never really took the time to express how grateful I am for all that you do for me and my son." She switched lanes. "Thank you for taking care of us when you didn't have to." She placed her hand out and touched my leg. "My loyalty lay with you, so don't ever think I'll cross you."

"That's what a real man is supposed to do. He provides for those that he cares for, baby girl." I placed my left hand on top of hers. "And if I had to question your loyalty, believe me, you wouldn't be around me. Remember that!" Finding a parking spot at Coney Island was always hard to find, but somehow we were in luck. Just as a car pulled out in front of us, we slid right in the spot. "Ready to have some fun?" I asked shorty as I tucked the gat under my black Tee.

"I only came out here for some funnel cake," she said laughing her ass off.

"What?" I smiled seeing her happy and free.

"The baby got me craving for it." She walked around to meet me. "I want a girl." She let me know right off top.

"I Just want a healthy baby." I reached for her hand.

****

I played almost every game that there was to play. All Pound wanted to do was collect the gifts and eat. She had about four plates of funnel cake already.

"You ready to bounce?" I asked her as I helped out with all the stuffed animals I'd won.

"I guess." She pouted.

"Next time, we'll bring the boys and stay longer."

"Promise?"

"Word, I had a good time." That got a smile out of her.

An eerie feeling washed over me the closer and closer we got to the Audi. I sensed someone watching us. I was strapped and ready to let that muthafucka bark. Fuck these muthafuckin' people out this bitch. I put all the bags in my left hand as my right hand reached up the back of my shirt. I walked Pound Cake around to the driver's side. I heard screeching tires and I pulled my toolie out racing for the other side. Screams rang, but the sound of gun fire rang louder.

Boom! Boom! Boom! Boom! Boom! I clapped back staring dead at Cuba. What these bitches thought I wasn't going to bust back. Ain't no pussy in my blood. The Denali swerved as a young nigga's body hung out the back window.

"*Trap!*" Pound Cake screamed opening the car door, but fuck that. I was ready to end this nigga today and I fucked the trigger again.

"*You pussy!*" I screamed as I kept finger fucking the trigger. *Boom! Boom*! The hit sent my body in the car.

Jamaica

"Argghhh!" I hollered out from the pain as I kept my pussy finger on the trigger.

"*Oh my God! Oh my God, you're bleeding!*" she screamed as she sped away.

I leaned up checking the rearview mirror to see if they were following us, but they weren't. I held the spot I felt the blood leaking, as I kept my eyes in the mirror.

"Just keep driving!" I leaned my head back on the headrest. "Call, Rocket—fuck!" I closed my was don't die, we muthafuckin" multiply. eyes trying my hardest to control my breathing. *Real niggas don't die, we muthafuckin' multiply.*

"Trap, Bae talk to me," I heard Pound Cake's voice, but I didn't respond.

Chapter 39

~Rocket~

I found Jae staring at our picture in our bedroom above our bed. "I'm sorry." I let out a long sigh. "I swear on my life, yo'."

She turned her head from the picture and looked at me with murder in her eyes. "You sorry? Sorry is for pussyclath succas, Draymond!"

I started to step toward her but she held her hand up stopping me. "I'm stressed to the max and your words pushed me to the edge today."

She laughed a devilish laugh. "So, you put your fucking hands on me again because of my mouth?" She laughed again but this time I got chills.

"Jae." I started walking again but I stopped as soon as I saw her pull the hammer from her waist. "I'm sorry," I pleaded to her.

"You muthafucka, I'm sorry!" She waved the gun around with her left hand on her stomach. "I'm sorry for loving you too fucking much!" She steadied the gun at my head. "To the point that I'll smoke anyone that hurts you or those that you love," she continued with tears in her eyes.

"Jae, I love you!" She tossed the burner on the bed closer to me.

"I killed that bitch!" She wiped her tears away.

"How and when?" I was happy that Cuba didn't get the chance to do that shit.

"When you went to Jersey, it was the perfect time."

I shook my head walking toward her. "Bae you had enough time to tell me." I walked up in her space. "I thought Cuba had done the hit, that's why I was so mad." I held her

Jamaica

face in my hands. "Your words hurt more than a bullet, bae." I kept talking not allowing her to reply to me. "Them muthafuckin' vows that I took with you, is for you and only you!" I tasted her tears on her lips. "I love you!"

She pushed me off her. "So, why the fuck you had to go see her body, if you love me so much, Rocket?"

"I didn't see her body, Jae." I gazed deep into her eyes. "I saw her mom."

She didn't say a word, but I knew she believed me. I had never lied to her and I had no plans to do so now.

"You need to figure out how we are going to tell, MiMi," she said as she walked away from me.

"I told you already." She picked her heater up tucking it back under her t-shirt. "You're going to help me."

The ringing of my phone barged in on our conversation. "Bruh, what's up?" I answered Trap's call.

"He's shot!"

I blinked my eyes. "What?" I snapped.

"*Yes!*" Pound Cake screamed.

"Aye, yo' calm down and talk to me. What happened?" I was on my way to the ride with Jae on my back as I listened to Pound Cake.

"Alright, meet me on Fulton Street."

"At that spot?" She knew the trap spot from Trap.

"Yeah, I'ma stay on the phone with you, though."

"Okay," she replied. "Trap!" she cried but I didn't hear him answer.

"Bae, call Goon and tell him Trap is hit and we on the way to Fulton Street. Have the doc there." She didn't reply, she did what I asked. "Pound Cake put me on speakerphone.

"Rocket, he is not talking."

I said a prayer to the man above to spare my brother's life. "Bruh, hold on." Tears danced from my eyes as I tried to stay calm and strong. "You can't do this shit to me, fam." I mashed the gas pedal down to the mat. I couldn't take losing the only nigga that I trusted my life and bitch around, I just couldn't.

"Trap, don't do this shit to me!" I heard Pound Cake crying harder.

Jae's touches usually made me feel good, but this time they felt cold.

Jamaica

Chapter 40

~Trap~

"A nigga gotta come harder than that to take a real muthafuckin' Shotta out, fam." I was laid up on a table in the trap house, as a bad bitch attended to my shoulder, while my brother stood to my right side. I felt nothing but when I glanced over at shorty working on my shoulder, I saw nothing but blood. "Muthafuckas thought I wasn't going to clap back, but them pussies don't know me, bruh."

A smile was plastered over Gotti's face when he saw me. "Truth!" He smiled wider.

"Cuba's bitch ass wasn't even blasting." I got mad all over again, replaying the incident in my head. "Over here," I pounded my chest with my right hand, "we all the way 'bout that life!"

"Bro." Rocket stepped up to me. "Calm down."

"*Calm down*, fuck no! The only way I'ma get calm, fam, is when that bitch is dead!"

****

Hours Later

I was in excruciating pain, all the medicine Gotti's nurse had given me had worn off. I damn sure wasn't talking anymore. "Fuck!" I gritted my teeth. "Mane, how the fuck you make it through all them shots, son?" I held my shoulder as I spoke to Rocket. "Shit—" He lifted the blunt up that he had prepared for us. "The same way you making it now, bro." He puffed the herb. "The only way we fall to death is from headshots." He handed me the blunt.

Jamaica

I couldn't help but think about my twin. My nigga was gone, but he'd always live forever with me. Tears welled up in my eyes, just thinking about how they did my blood. No matter how hard I tried to keep myself together, I couldn't. I let the tears descend. Rocket must have known what I was thinking and feeling cause the second I glanced over at him he was doing exactly what I was doing. Thugs Cry, too.

****

~Jae~

Trap was very adamant about not leaving Rocket's side till Cuba was dead. "Mane fuck all that shit, bro!" He raised hell when Rocket told him he needed some time to rest. "Because of that nigga we lost our brother for real," he voiced in front of everyone even the doctor.

If Cuba had continued to do business with us when Rocket got jammed, Tray wouldn't have linked up with the nigga that took his life.

"Take Pound Cake home and get the girls," Rocket said as Pound Cake spent some quality time with Trap. "And come right back, Jae."

"Anything else, Rocket?" I leaned my head to one side.

"You strapped?"

"Is my pussy always wet?"

"Always."

"So, you already know the answer then." He smiled.

Pound Cake and I wasn't the best of friends but I wouldn't deny the love that she had for Trap. I thought my blood Chessan really cared for him, but she didn't not from her actions.

"How are you feeling?" she asked me when I should have been the one asking her first.

"Okay," I rubbed my stomach. "And you?"

"I'm okay." She faced me with a sad look on her face. "But I'm worried."

"No need to be worried," I lied taking my eyes off the road for a split second to meet hers. "Dem deh rude boys nag uh leave weh."

"Huh?" We both laughed. She might not have understood, but I was just letting her know that them niggas wasn't going to leave us.

During the ride to Miss Judith's house, I got the chance to talk to Pound Cake one on one. She seemed really down to earth, loyal, and full of life. Someone Trap really needed to have on his team.

"I'm four weeks pregnant," she sang finally lightening up.

"Congrats!"

"Jae?" She took a second before she continued. "Thank you."

"No problem, if there is anything I can help out with don't second guess to hit me up." I gave her my number as I pulled up to Miss Judith's home.

****

Trap Jr. had grown so much since I had seen him last. He was a mirror reflection of his father. The girls were excited to see me along with their grandma, Miss Judith. Even though she wasn't Rocket's mother by blood, he was still hers. She loved him just as much as she loved her boys.

"How are you doing, baby?" She kissed my cheek.

Jamaica

"I'm good." Trap had made it real clear to me and his girl not to mention anything about him getting hit up to his mother. *She'll stress the fuck out,"* he barked. "And you?"

"I'm happy," she said looking around the room at her family. "Where are my boys?"

"Out taking care of business," I lied straight to her face, I had to.

Within twenty minutes I was back at home with the girls. Rocket was waiting up for us. "Look at my queens."

"Daddy," MiMi sang running to him.

Moo was at that age where she was finding herself, and Rocket knew that. He didn't want them to grow up. As soon as MiMi was in his arms, he tickled her as she begged him to stop. Moments like these were priceless and I couldn't wait to feel that same love toward my son. Me and Moo took a seat beside each other, she reached for her phone and I reached for the remote.

"I have something I have to say." Rocket had Mimi on his lap.

"Okay." MooMoo put her phone down.

I took a deep breath as I waited on Rocket to continue. "Something happened to your mom, MiMi." He stared at his heart.

Her eyes popped and my trigger finger itched, wishing I could do that bitch over again for hurting her.

"What?" Moo asked.

"She went away." He paused looking over at me. "And she is not coming back."

"Good!" Moo said with a straight face. "My sister don't need her."

"She not coming back?" MiMi asked with a puppy's sad face. Ashanti had hurt her, but MiMi still loved her.

"No, baby." Rocket held her. "I know, I'm not your mom." I got up and walked toward them. "But I promise, I'll love you more than she did."

"Promise?"

"Cross my heart." I did it with my trigger finger. I'll pull it for this family any day. "On everything that I love!"

Baby girl got off her daddy's lap and hugged me with so much love I couldn't stop the tears from falling.

Jamaica

Chapter 41

~Rocket~

A few days later, Miss Pam buried her daughter. I didn't allow MiMi to attend, and her grandma Pam thought it was an okay decision.

"I'm not going to keep MiMi away from you." I was out making moves when I placed the call. "I'm not that type of person."

"Thank you, Draymond."

"Miss Pam, any time you want to see her just hit me up and you'll see her."

When Ashanti used to beef with me over our child, her mother always saw otherwise.

"Boss," Beam addressed me from the backseat because the passenger seat was taken up by Trap.

No matter how much I preached to that nigga to stay home he just couldn't.

"Niggas low out here," Beam continued. "We missing out on hella bread."

"Give me a few days, G." I started the Audi up. "Shit will be back normal soon."

"Bet that." He extended his fist up and I fist-bumped him.

Once Beam exited the car, I pulled off in Scarface's direction, until I got a call from Goon.

"Boss, where you at?"

"Out and about. What's good, gangsta?"

"Swing my way." Excitement filled his tone. "Cuz you not gonna believe this shit!"

"Say no more." I dropped the call.

Trap was mad quiet, he had yet to say a word about anything.

"You straight, Bruh."

"Yeah, just got a lot on my mind, fam," he replied.

"Poke ya chest out." I turned the radio off. "We family, bruh."

"You right," he agreed and with that my bruh said what was on his chest. He had fallen really hard for Chessan, and he found out she had a whole nigga over there in the UK with her.

"What? Jae didn't even mention that shit to me," I let him know. "That's her fam, bruh," he said.

"So what, nigga! You her family, too. You know blood is just blood, everyone bleeds that shit, but loyalty is family with us."

"You right—" he paused. "—but anyway I tried to hit her up and a nigga hit me back."

"Hell nah!"

"Mane, I told that nigga keep that hitch!"

I couldn't help but laugh, but I could tell that he was really fucked up over Jae's sister. "Don't let ya emotions get the best of you to the point that you can't concentrate out in these streets, Bruh."

"Mane, that bitch is history. Chessan who?" We laughed together. "I'ma wife Pound up."

"That's a good move, bruh. Shorty loves you."

I'd seen and heard the way she goes all out for Trap and that's exactly what he needed in his corner. Someone that would weather the storm with him no matter what the temperature. I thanked God daily for Jae, wifey was the fucking truth.

****

"I'm in your hood. Where you at, B?" I questioned Goon.

"I'm looking dead at you, Bossman."

I looked around but I didn't spot youngin' at all.

"Drive four houses down, fam."

I put the car in gear and within seconds I spotted Goon standing on the porch of a brick house. Trap exited the car like he hadn't got hit up a few days ago.

"What's good, bruh?" Goon nodded his head toward Trap.

"Chillin," he responded as he looked around the block.

"What's crackin', son?" I asked

"Take a walk with me," said Goon.

He led the way in the house and down the steps until we were in the basement. The crib was empty except for a few chairs.

"What the fuck?" I asked Goon staring at a light skin mixed nigga tied up in front of us.

"Ain't this some shit!" Trap announced walking around me in the direction of the captive. "Cuba's runner."

"What bro?" I was standing beside my brother.

"This the pussy that tried to take me out the other day."

"Huh?" I questioned, wondering how the fuck did this nigga even get here.

Bloodstained the white tile floor. The boy's head was resting on the wall, his eyes were shut from straight blows. He was now black and purple.

"So, I get this call saying how a nigga trying to spend some hella bread, and he wanted to hook up with me," Goon replayed the event. Goon asked one of his runners how much the person wanted, so when he got the message back stating that they wanted ten birds, he knew something wasn't right then. "I don't sell that type of weight, Bossman," he continued. "Then my peoples said dude was traveling in something that looked mad familiar. That had his attention on the move. So, he got two of the runners to meet up with ole

Jamaica

boy. Come to find out another ride was trailing them from a distance. They didn't panic, fam," Goon praised his crew. "You remember Skip, right?"

"Hell yeah!" Cuba had caught Goon's goons slipping and Skip was one of them.

"Well, his little brother Clappa with me now."

"Okay." I nodded as I listened to the story. I didn't want to miss anything.

"Clappa and Mani told ole boy—" He pointed at the pussy in front of us. "—to follow us, which he did. The whole time Clappa and Mani was doing their end, me and Brad started following the other ride. That's when I saw Cuba in the passenger seat."

"What?" I rubbed my hands together, realizing that Cuba was on a real mission to wipe me out. "Mane that pussy wasn't ready. I made more bullets rain than I ever did money in the strip club, fam." I smiled, now it was my time to be made proud. "Once my goons got this nigga inside everything else was a cupcake."

Bam! I jammed the nigga in the face with my hammer.

"Argghhh," he hollered out in pain.

"Wake the fuck up!" I jammed him again.

"Bruh, let me handle this one!" Trap expressed.

I moved out of his way.

Chapter 42

~Trap~

I went back to the ride just to make sure everything was at a standstill outside but Brad was posted up with his eyes dancing around.

"You straight, B?"

"I'm a hunnid, fam," he replied showing me two hammers.

I moved back through the crib with a purpose and a plan in mind. This was our ticket straight to Cuba, fuck chasing that nigga. *Bam! Bam!* I fired my fist off on the pussy. Pain shot through my body especially my shoulder, but I pushed through it. *Bam!* My left hand connected to his jaw.

"Arrggghhh!" he hollered out coughing up blood.

The chair that held him flipped on its side with his body still in it.

"Help me pick this pussy up, bro?" I asked Rocket. "Muthafucka you tried to take me out, huh?" I had my face all up in the nigga's face.

"It was—" he whined in pain. "—an order."

"An order by, Cuba?" I barked as beads of sweat dripped from my forehead. "Huh?" I asked again, but he didn't respond. I pulled the burner from under my shirt.

His eyes popped wide open. "Yes." He coughed and blood leaked from his mouth.

"How can I find him?" I stood back.

"I can't tell—" He took a long breath. "—you, he'll kill my whole family."

"So, you rather die over a muthafucka that doesn't give a fuck about you?" Rocket voiced.

"Facts!" *Click! Clack*! I jammed a bullet in the head.

Jamaica

"If that nigga cared anything about you, B, he would be blazing fire through the streets right now for you," Rocket continued. "Listen, you don't even hear nothing, bruh. Let me tell you some real shit youngin." Rocket stepped closer to him. "If my nigga, my right-hand man got caught up and had been missing for days, this whole muthafuckin' city would be filled with chalk lines."

I knew Rocket's mind frame. He wanted youngin' to realize that Cuba should have been made a move. But Cuba wasn't no real muthafuckin' gangsta. Yes, his money was long but that was it. That nigga don't put in no work, he don't buss his gun for his team. Behind his crew, he's a straight-up, bitch.

"Bruh, fuck that shit you spittin'!" I placed the pistol against youngin's forehead. "This nigga love Cuba's life more than his own."

Chapter 43
~Jae~

"Jae, wah a gwaan," my father said as soon as I answered his call. "I'm good and you?"

"When last you talked to, Chessan?"

I stopped washing the dishes, cause the tone my father was using had me feeling some type of way. "The last time she called was the last time I chatted with her." My patwah was coming out. "Weh yuh really call meh fa?" I wanted him to cut the bullshit and get to the point.

"A yuh sista."

"I know she is my sister. And?"

"You are supposed to ride with her on everything."

"Ride with her on everything, huh?" I laughed. "Hell no," I answered. "Fuck no." This was my first time cursing to my father. "I don't give a fuck if she is my blood or not."

"Excuse me?" he said.

"With me, it's loyalty over everything even my own bloodclath blood!" I hung the call up.

Chessan's last words to me were, "*Fuck you!*"

That's exactly how I was carrying it with her and since my father was on her side, it was fuck him, too.

Jamaica

Chapter 44
~Rocket~

"Alright! Alright! I'll talk." Youngin' cracked under pressure, straight pussy.

I looked over at Goon and he was shaking his head from side to side with a disgusted look on his face. He was probably thinking how youngin' wasn't the same nigga now that he was when he was bussin' that heat.

Trap slowly pulled the hammer away with a smile on his face. "I need to know everything," he gritted, with death in his eyes. "If you lie you don't have to worry about Cuba finding your family because I'll find them first."

Twenty minutes later, the pussy told us everything about Cuba and all we needed to know. "I'ma check all that shit out, and if it's true I'll let you live," I said, then walked toward Goon. "Keep an eye on that nigga at all times," I commanded.

"Say no more, bro, but I'm moving on that trip with you to find Cuba."

Cuba had taken two of his brothers from him. All he wanted to do was see to it that Cuba got what he had dished out, and that was death. I couldn't deny Goon the right to pay homage to his niggas. "I already counted you in gangsta," I said with respect.

****

Fuck giving that pussy time to collect his thoughts. His team was getting shorter and shorter fucking with me and my shottas. Jae had cooked dinner and had the girls already tucked away when we got to the crib.

"Tonight's the night, baby."

Jamaica

"For what'?" She sat up on the sofa as Trap headed for the basement. "You'll see when I get back."

"I'll be waiting," she said getting up. She was getting bigger and bigger each day. I couldn't wait to meet my little nigga.

"Come back to us, Rocket." She kissed me and placed her hand on my heart. "Please."

****

Cuba's soldier gave up his main location when Trap clapped a bullet in the chamber. Nigga were quick to scream how loyal they are, but as soon as that pressure touches, they start singing like hummingbirds. It was Ice, Goon, Trap and myself on this trip. I had to have those extra eyes with me. The Bronx was where Cuba lived, so the ride was nothing major. Once I hit White Plains Road I knew shit was really real.

"I hope that pussy ain't lie," Goon spoke up.

"And if he did, I'ma make that muthafucka bleed," Trap clapped back.

As we pulled up on Cuba's street, I spotted two of his rides off top. Yeah, we were at the right spot. I glanced over at my brother marching right beside me with a smile.

"I'ma take the front with, Trap. You and Goon hit the buck." Ice bobbed his head understanding me all the way. "Leave no one alive!" The majority of the lights were on in the house. "Bruh, you ready?" I asked Trap before he hit the lawn.

"Been ready, fam!"

Ice and Goon took off to the back. Cameras lined each angle of his crib but we didn't care. *Blocka! Blocka! Blocka!* The Mac-II spit heat from my fingertip at the front door. Gotti had reached out and got in touch with the Chief for the Bronx Police Department and hit him off with some bread.

Blocka! Blocka! Blocka! Bullets filled the front door like the *Connect Four* game making it easier to gain access. *Boom!* I kicked the door and the wood snapped opening it up. The first floor was empty of bodies but not bullet holes. This muthafucka was living like Scarface. Chandeliers hung from the ceiling throughout the first floor.

"I'ma hit upstairs," Trap said but I was tagging along with him.

That was the plan.

"We don't move without each other," I reminded him. *Blocka! Blocka!* "What the fuck?" We dashed behind the sofa for cover not knowing where the shots were coming from.

"On four," I said, motioning with my hand, "we're blazing."

Trap nodded his understanding. I peeked my head out and saw two Hispanic men with hammers coming down the stairs. "Mi amigo!" One of them screamed.

"Cuba!" the other yelled.

I shook my head and me and Trap stood up sending pure heat their way, straight to the head. Blocka! Blocka! Their bodies rocked before they came crashing down the stairs. We climbed over the bodies and made our way up the stairs. Cuba had a game room, movie room, bar and everything upstairs.

"That nigga not here, bruh." I felt defeated not finding Cuba. The entire upstairs was empty. "That muthafucka gonna know we were here, though!"

My phone rang, and it was Gotti, so I answered. "You, have ten minutes, youngin', make it quick!"

"Already."

I dropped the call heading back downstairs. "Look who we ran into," Goon's voice sang.

"Muthafucka leaving out the back door, O.G.," Ice added.

"Hola." I stepped down the stairs, mean-mugging his friend that I knew all too well. "Longtime, Ricardo," I addressed Ro's bitch ass father, the nigga that got my father life behind them walls.

"Fuck you!" he spat.

"Fuck me, huh?" *Boom*! I hit his shoulder. *Boom*! I found his knee and he fell right at my feet. "You just a bitch like your son." I stood over him as he curled up in pain.

"I should have killed you." He stared up at me in contempt.

"You didn't and you never will!" *Blocka! Blocka*! I hit his mental all the way up.

Cuba tried to make a run for it, but Trap sat that ass back with a slug. "Argghhh!" he hollered out.

"He ain't that gangsta without his team!" Goon spoke up. "You killed my brothers, pussy!" He shot Ricardo Sr. in the leg.

"You cause my bro to get slumped up," Trap mentioned as he touched Cuba's stomach with a slug.

Cuba kept hollering out but gun fire covered up the weak noises he was making. "Pussy!" I shot four slugs into his chest.

His eyes stared up at us in surprise. "Fuck you!"

I stepped back so Ice could finish the muthafucka that caused me hell.

Chapter 45

~Rocket~

"The coast is clear." I hit Gotti's line as we were in the ride.

"I thought you had planned to stay the night?" Gotti announced with a chuckle.

"Mane, that bitch ass nigga Ricardo was in attendance," I broke the news to Gotti.

"*Ricardo?*" he questioned me with a solid tone.

"Ro's bitch ass father, the pussy that got my father jammed up." I got mad all over thinking about how that nigga did my ole man dirty.

"What?"

"Yeah, that nigga had to be a good friend of Cuba's. He was in his crib with him."

"Damn!" Gotti expressed as I told him the story. "This is going to be great news to deliver to your father."

"I know it will!"

We stopped on the way back at Goon's brick house where We had the youngin' at.

"You good from here, OG?" Ice asked me when we were outside.

'Yeah, I'm straight OG." I dapped him up. "And thank you." I released him from my embrace.

"Nothin' but love Rocket." He started to step away from the ride.

"Let me get you home."

"I'm good, youngsta." He disappeared into the night.

Trap was standing on the steps of the house with Goon as I watched Ice until he was out of my sight.

"Let's end this party, yo!" I said walking toward them.

Jamaica

Cuba's goon was barely alive when we entered the basement. Brad was posted up in the corner with a blunt hanging out of his mouth.

"What's good?" he greeted us with a mouth full of smoke.

"Take a walk with me, bruh," Goon told his homie.

****

~Trap~

Bam! I jammed that nigga with the heater.

"Arrgghhhh!" he hollered out in pain.

"Your information was on point." I crouched down so I could be eye level with the nigga. "But ya life is still mine," I let the half-dead nigga know straight up.

Ole boy's eyes flicked open as he gave it his all to lean his head up. "But you promised me—" his words were spaced out and low. "—that I would live."

My loyalty didn't lie with a nigga that tried his hardest to kill me. This nigga had the game all the way fucked up. I'll never let a muthafucka live that tried to kill me. I damn sure didn't give a fuck that he told me everything about Cuba to save himself. I stood up and watched as his body tensed up, he knew what time it was.

Boom! Boom!

Chapter 46

~Jae~

Seeing Rocket and Trap standing in front of me gave me a peace I couldn't describe. I thanked the man above for their protection.

"Ice and Goon?" I stood to my feet as I studied their faces.

"They safe!" Trap answered before he walked off.

"Anything you ever ask me for, you will get it." Rocket stood in my space, dropped a duffle bag at my feet and kissed my forehead before he left me. His swagger alone turned me on so much that I wanted to chase him down and fuck his brains out.

I unzipped the bag and smiled as my pussy jumped. I picked the bag up and carried it to my car with a smile on my face. A short while later we were at home, and Rocket was climbing in the shower.

"Can I join you?" I took all my clothes off not waiting for Rocket to respond. Seeing his dick jump, I knew I was invited to take a shower with him. I was already soaking wet from his gangsta.

"Oh, my god!" I grabbed his dick as the hot water splashed over our bodies. "I want you!" I purred.

"I need you!" Rocket groaned and rubbed my stomach, biting down on his bottom lip.

"Baby, meh need yuh, now," I begged as I leaned my head back and lifted one of my legs up. "Rocket put it in," I whined but my king ignored my request as he dropped to his knees, bowing down to his pussy. "Oui wee," I cried out in pleasure holding onto his head as his mouth danced back and forth over my pussy. Sweet tears mixed with water ran down my body as I held on for the ride. "Rocket!" My legs wobbled.

Jamaica

"Rocket!" I cried, but he didn't stop, he pushed his face harder and deeper into my ocean as I splashed my juices down his mouth. "Argghhh!" I gripped his head as my body jerked back and forth. "Fuck!" I closed my eyes tight, praying that I wouldn't fall the fuck out. Rocket ate my pussy like it was a plate of oxtails and butter beans with rice and peas.

He pulled back and said, "I never ever want you to forget who you belong to." I couldn't ignore his statement. My heart, mind, body, and soul belonged to him and I had to remind him.

"I'll kill myself before I let anyone get what belongs to you."

His dick was so hard that when I grabbed it, the veins stood out. Rocket picked me up and placed me against the wall. My legs instantly wrapped around his waist.

"Yasss!" I screamed inside his collar bone to drown out the excitement he caused when he let the tip of his dick slap against my clit.

"You want it?" he teased as the wall and his body held me up. "Huh?" he whispered, but I didn't have the strength to come up with an answer that he already knew. "Tell me you want this dick." He rubbed over my hole, teasing me to the highest level that there was. "Tell me, Jae."

I picked my head up so I could gaze into his eyes. I wanted him to feel my words and understand that no matter where he was, or what he was doing I didn't just need him. I had to have him and I was only safe with him and only him.

"Draymond." I blinked and the tears raced down my cheeks as I stared into his eyes, emotions had me, but only Rocket could cause them to fill me up. "Not only do I want you to put it in, but I need you to comprehend that without you there is no me. I love you with every fiber in my body." He smiled, but I needed him to understand how deep my love ran for him. "If you were to ever leave me, I promise you on our son's life, I would die."

He kissed away my tears, and my body relaxed in his arms. "Now can you please fuck me?" I braced myself. "Oh, my gosh!" My body arched as he entered me. "Fuck!" He licked my ear as I bit my bottom lip, with each thrust my body rocked in his arms as he touched my soul.

If loving Rocket was wrong, I'd kill every muthafucka who had the heart to say it, cause there wasn't any other loving that could compete with his. As he nibbled on my left ear and gave me long strokes my body shook.

"Got damn!" I voiced as I dug my fingers into his back. Pound after pound, my body stiffened up as my eyes clamped shut.

"Let me see your eyes," he begged as my head leaned against the tile, but I didn't comply with his request, so he stopped moving.

"Rocket, really?" I opened my eyes to see a smile plastered over his handsome face.

"I wanna see you bust, baby," he demanded. "With your eyes open."

He started to move his hips again, but this time slower. The way his body swayed, it felt like he hadn't stopped seconds ago. Each stroke caused my legs to clutch tighter and tighter in a stiff lock behind his back. My heart pounded as if the boys in blue were chasing me. My back arched and my toes clamped like a closed fist.

"Rocket," I sang out with my eyes staring into his.

"Splash 'em juices over this dick," his voice demanded as he dug deeper inside of me gazing into my soul. "Cum for, daddy." His hip pulled back. "Now, Jae!" He rammed deep into me.

Jamaica

I clawed away at his back as my eyes rolled in my head. My mouth was wide open as my tongue traveled around my lips, and my inner walls gripped his dick. The nut started in my toes and moved up my legs. "Argghh," a small cry escaped from my mouth. My heart stopped beating as I closed my eyes. Fuck that shit Rocket was spitting about me keeping my eyes open.

"That's what I'ma aim for forever till God calls me home," he said with a smile covering his face as he lowered my body. "But I gotta make you pay for not listening to me." He chuckled.

"Make me pay in our bedroom," I suggested.

"Say no more!" He washed my body from head to toe before he did his.

"I love you!" I said as I stepped into our room.

"I love you more, Mrs. Wallace!" Rocket beat my body sore for an hour nonstop. Every position there was he had my ass twisted into one like I wasn't months away from giving birth to our son. "Damn!" I expressed after he had busted all up in me. He pulled my body toward his and said something I couldn't understand. "What?" I questioned. But nothing came from him. He had worn himself out completely. I closed my eyes and let the words flow from my lips. "Lord, thank you for another day. Thank you for protecting my family." I rubbed Rocket's chest. "Keep us strong, keep us safe, in your name I pray, Amen."

****

I was swagged out when I left the house. Dressed in an all-gray Adidas top and bottom cuffed my pregnant body to the T. The white high-top Air Force Ones graced my feet, as I rocked a high wraparound ponytail bun. I was fresh to death with my toolie resting on my waist beside my belly. I dialed Ribbon's number as I tossed the duffle bag in the trunk of the car. I had taken it inside with me earlier, simply as a precaution.

"You at work?" I asked as soon as she picked up.

"Yeah," she replied.

"Bet dat!" I ended the call as I entered the car.

It didn't take me more than fifteen minutes to pull up at Ribbon's job.

"Rib," I greeted her at the front door of her business.

"Sis!" She smiled covering up her mouth as she stared at my big ass stomach.

"How are you?" I hugged her.

"Oh, my gosh!" She let me go to stare at my stomach. "Auntie Rib loves you." She talked to D.J.

Even though she wasn't my blood, she was my sista. Her loyalty was that and for that alone. I'll give her nothing but love and loyalty in return.

"And I love you back, Auntie," I responded back sounding like a baby.

"Girl, pregnancy has you glowing." She held my hand smiling.

"I can't wait to have this boy." We walked inside toward her office.

"Sis, you just in time," she said as she opened her door. I smelled the food the moment the knob turned, and my stomach growled. "Pancakes, eggs, bacon, and sausage. I just had IHOP delivered to me right before you pulled up."

"Girl, thank God, cause I'm starving." That workout Rocket gave me had my stomach touching my back.

Rib split the breakfast right down the middle. "Grab a bottle of water from the fridge." Rib pointed across the room.

Jamaica

I got up and got two bottles. "I'll drink the water. You can drink the orange juice." She was so considerate.

"Sis, believe me, I swallow more vitamins than a store sales."

"You a nasty bitch!"

We both busted out laughing. We chopped it up about everything between bites. Her girls were doing well as she raised them as a single parent.

"You never reached out to my brother, did you?" She had given T.T. her number but he never mentioned to me if she had called or not.

"Truth be told, Jae." She took a sip of the orange juice. "I'm not ever going to get over my husband." Sadness washed over her face as she thought about Rich for a flash moment. "I miss him so damn much," she continued as a tear rolled down her left cheek. "Only thing I can live on is the memories that we shared and our girls that we created in love."

I watched as her eyes traveled across the room to land on a family photo. "Believe me he's fucking proud of you, Rib." I sat my empty plate down and reached for my sista's hand. She stood to her feet and I wiped her tears away. "You have two angels that you have to be strong for." I stared into her eyes. "You're doing a great job raising them by yourself, Rib."

Her tears ran rapidly down her face like a storm. "Thank you." She embraced me. "Thank you for being here for me, Jae," she said between sobs.

"No need to thank me." I pulled back so I could glance into her eyes. "It's all love with us, baby girl." Our bond was unbreakable, what we had created could only be destroyed by one of us, no one else.

"I love you, girl." She held my shoulders.

"Meh luv yuh tu, Rib."

As she cleaned up from our breakfast, I ran the story down to her about Ashanti.

"What?" she snapped when I got to the point of how Ashanti had beat MiMi up. "I know you gave her the business," she sang dumping the plastic trays into the trash can.

"A yardi babies weh be, suh yuh already know." I winked at her as I tried to get up, but she stopped me with the hand motion.

"Yeah, mon, meh know."

We laughed and talked for a few hours nonstop, times like these were priceless and nothing else mattered at the moment to me. Seeing a smile on Rib's face was all that and more.

"Girl!" I checked my phone to see if I had missed any calls but I didn't. "Let me get back home before Rocket puts out an amber alert out for me," I said getting up.

"We have to do this more," Rib stated.

"Yes, we do," I agreed.

Once I got to my ride with Rib at my side, I popped the trunk. "This is yours." I pointed at the duffle bag that Rocket had dropped at my feet last night.

"Mine?" she questioned.

"Yup, go ahead and check it out." A confused look danced over her face. I watched as she unzipped the bag then spread it open. A foul scent traveled out, but it didn't affect us. "You wanted that pussyclot's head on a platter, right?" Her eyes didn't stagger away from the bag until I touched her hand. "I told you, I'm my sista's keeper till they bury me."

"Jae," she mumbled. "Thank you!"

Ice had dismantled Cuba's head from his body so I handed it over to my bitch as she had requested. "Thank you," she voiced picking the bag up from my trunk.

"You need some help?"

"Help?" She smiled. "You did enough, Jae." She walked off toward her chop shop.
"Make sure you hit me up!" I yelled closing the trunk.

Chapter 47

~Rocket~

"Rocket, wake up!" Jae screamed gripping my hand. I jumped up reaching for my tool. "Oh, my God!" she hollered out breathing hard as fuck holding her stomach.

The fear from thinking someone was trying to catch us slipping vanished when I realized that my wife was in labor. "Bae relax," I tried to coach her but the look she gave me stopped my lips from saying anything more. I got a quick glance at my watch it was two p.m. I had just closed my eyes minutes ago.

"Get-me-tu-deh-hospital!" The lock she had on my hand had me stepping. Pain was displayed all over her face.

"Jae, breathe," I reminded her as we took baby steps.

No one was home but us, the girls were at school. Trap was with Pound Cake.

Jae's palm got wet instantly and sweat formed on her forehead. "Uggghhh!"

"You a, G," I let her know.

She stopped walking toward the garage. "You ain't feeling this muthafuckin pain that's rocking through my body." Her grip got stronger. Even though she was in mad pain her mouth still rang shots.

****

~Jae~

All the shit Rocket was spitting about breathing made me even more vexed. I'd rather take another bullet than feel this pain. Contractions rocked my body back and forth as I held on to my seat.

"Bae!" Rocket switched between cars like a race car driver. "We are almost there."

"Arrgghhh." I leaned my head back, trying my best not to lift my legs up and start pushing the little nigga out. "A weh deh bloodclath!" I punched the dashboard as I held my breath.

Rocket slammed the car in park as my body jerked forward. I didn't have the chance to cuss him out he was out the door at full speed. Seconds passed that felt like hours before Rocket opened my door with a wheelchair and two nurses.

"Call my doctor," I advised him as I got in the chair.

"I'm on it, bae."

Chapter 48

~Trap~

"How about we get married?" PoundCake suggested as I held her body after a long morning of lovemaking.

"*Married*?" I questioned, really questioning myself. Was I ready for that shit?

"You heard me." She pushed my chest trying to get away from me but I held her tightly, but not for long cause my phone started ringing.

"What's good nigga?" I greeted Rocket seeing his name flashing across my screen.

"Man, bruh," Rocket said with anxiety. "Jae is in labor."

"What?" I said sitting up in the bed. I kept the phone at my ear as I mouthed to Pound Cake that Jae was in labor.

"Hell yeah, son!" Excitement echoed from my brother's voice.

"Where is, MiMi and Moo?" I questioned as I got up to get dressed.

"Mom about to pick them up from school. Jae is almost at ten centimeters," his mouth ran. "I'm 'bout to be a dad again."

"Yeah, for the third time." I laughed.

"Son, you right behind me." He cracked up. "I gotta go fam, can't afford to miss this son."

"Shit, you better not. Fucking with Jae you won't live to tell the story." We shared a laugh together.

"Rocket," I continued. "Congrats, fam."

"Thanks, bro." He dropped the call.

Pound Cake staggered in front of me in her bra and panties and I couldn't help but pull her into my arms. Her stomach was growing faster than anything I know that could expand.

"Jae is in labor." I sniffed her hair.

"I heard," she responded with a smile on her face.

I was so happy that I didn't let her slip through the crack of my hands. The whole time I was looking for a gem and didn't recognize that I had her already.

"Let's get dressed so we can see our niece." I kissed her forehead.

It's been a month and a half since we've been living together with our boys under our own roof. There wasn't a night that went by that I wasn't home with my boys and my bitch. The streets still had me but since Cuba was gone, shit was a lot easier. The money was coming in by the double as we continued to supply Brooklyn.

Chapter 49

~Rocket~

At 4:17 p.m., Jae gave birth to our son D.J. He weighed 8lbs 4oz, stretching out at 22inches long. Jae pushed my boy out without any medicine to ease her pain. Rude gal was the truth, she had shown it over and over again. Little man looked just like me, all Jae did was carry him. He had curly hair that covered his ears, long fingers and a rustic look of a gangsta like me written all over his face.

"Damn!" Trap said when he arrived. "Mane, that's your twin."

The girls were in love with their brother at first sight. Miss Judith catered to Jae making sure she was okay as everyone gave D.J. all the attention.

"Thank you," I whispered in her ear when everyone was gone.

"No, thank you." She held our son in her arms with pure love. Her eyes watered as she stared at DJ. "I'll love you forever and ever," she said as she leaned her head down and kissed his forehead.

****

~Jae~

Feeling the pressure gone from between my legs I knew my son was out but seeing him in my doctor's hand gave me some peace. When Rocket cut the umbilical cord, I knew love was real right then. I would never turn my back on my child, like my parents did, *never*. The second D.J. touched my hand, my heart pumped and the tears I had inside escaped from my

Jamaica

eyes easily. Tears to protect him for life, tears of joy. Our bond was already strong when I found out that he was growing inside of me, but now our bond would be until death and beyond anything or anyone I've ever loved. I stayed in the hospital for three days with Rocket at my side with our son. Ice was on deck just in case. The real close goons of Rocket stopped by to show the prince of ours some mad love.

"I'm so happy to be home," I said as I walked into our house. The girls were still with Miss Judith. "I need a blunt," I voiced.

Rocket laughed out loud. "Really?" Rocket said carrying DJ in the car seat over to the sofa.

"Shit, I'm not breastfeeding, rude boi." I danced a little just imaging the blunt on my lips. "You said I was hating when I was pregnant and couldn't blaze, but shit, you hating hard now." I twisted my lips up.

"You funny, yo'." He walked toward me with that gangsta walk.

Even though I was bleeding my body still craved for him. I belonged to him, I was his mind, body, and soul.

"I love you!" He gripped my face staring down at me.

I felt the wood on my leg jump, and since D.J. was asleep and it had been days since Rocket let one go. I thought right now was the perfect time. Since my pussy was out of commission my hands and mouth had to clock in for work.

"I love you more!" I let my hands roam down into his jeans gripping the steel.

"You want smoke?" his voice cracked.

"I'm 'bout that life, so let me blow you out." Down I went as he braced himself against the wall. Two minutes later I had Rocket pulling my hair from my roots. "Damn!" I got up re-pinning my ponytail up as I licked my lips from top to bottom.

"You can't handle my smoke, rude boi," I said walking off to my son.

    Rocket had yet to move, his head was against the wall with his eyes shut. My head game had him stuck.

Jamaica

Chapter 50

~Rocket~

Two Weeks Later

OX was granted a retrial in his case. His lawyers were present along with the District Attorney as we awaited the news at home. I had talked to my pops earlier that morning.

"How you feeling, OG?" I asked him.

"No feelings son, it is what it is," he responded. "I can't live in the past. If it's meant to be it will be—" he paused. "How is the family?"

"Good." I didn't tell him that everyone would be at my house as we waited on the news that would change our lives forever.

"Well, I'll link you when I hear something," he said.

"Do that ole man."

"Bet."

****

Gotti was pacing the floor, PoundCake and Jae were in the kitchen. Miss Judith had D.J. in her arms feeding him. The kids were playing in their rooms. Trap was looking out the window as I watched the news, waiting on the verdict about my pops. The second Gotti's phone rang, I stood up as he stopped pacing.

"Hello," he answered, hitting the speaker button so we all could listen.

"Sir," the lawyer started off the conversation. "A whole lot happened," the lawyer continued. "There were a lot of facts and a lot of fiction." Gotti shook his head. "They called the main witness to take the stand to testify but according to the D.A. the witness was deceased."

Miss Judith's eyes were closed as she burped D.J.

"Who was the witness?" Gotti asked.

"Ricardo Johnson Sr. Does the name ring any bells?"

"No," Gotti answered off the rip. We knew that fuck nigga.

"Anyway, due to not having the main witness to testify the case couldn't hold court." I held my breath and for the first time in my life, I felt like I was going to pass out. "He is set to be free at 3:30 p.m. today!"

Gotti grabbed me and I embraced him back. A smile was on mom's face. "Thank you," Gotti's voice sang in my ear.

Jae and Pound Cake entered the room. I let Gotti go and reached for my rock, my queen, my heart. I buried my face inside her collar bone as her hands wrapped around my back.

"Finally!" I mumbled.

My father was finally a free man. The entire family took the trip to pick up my OG. As we waited on him to emerge through the gates of hell. I held my son with Miss Judith standing beside me and Gotti on the other side. The rest of the family stayed in the vehicles. My ole man was a youngin' when he caught that fucked up case. He had been gone almost my entire life. Twenty-seven years later and he was getting a taste of life again.

When the gates open and I saw my pops walking toward me, I held my son tighter. OX would get the chance to be a grandfather in flesh. Even though he was a dad from behind the walls, now I had him in person. Miss Judith stepped forward, and I could tell that she was dreaming and floating all in one. My OG was tall and solid, his height towered over Ma Dukes. They shared a moment before Gotti walked up and invaded their space. The loyalty and love they had between them was identical to what me and Trap shared. Gotti wiped his eyes and right then and there I saw death before dishonor in flesh.

"Thank you," my old man told Gotti.

"If the shoe was on the other foot, I know the love and loyalty would have been the same. So, fuck that thank you shit."

They shared another hug before he started walking again. "My son," I read his lips.

"Dad," I voiced. "Welcome home." Our embrace was magical, three generations together finally.

****

Weeks Later

Miss Judith was the happiest woman in the world. My ole man made sure she was standing beside him where she belonged. Trap and Pound Cake got married. My nigga gave the game up and invested his money into a construction company called Tray Starz after his Twin. He got the warrant that the NYPD had out on him fixed. No witness, no case.

"Bruh, you know if you ever need me you know I'm coming blazing. Death before Dishonor, Loyalty over Everything," he preached from his heart.

"Already!"

Me and Goon touched Scarface, removing him out of the picture forever. I placed Brad in charge and monitored how the little young nigga moved. The money was always straight, and he was 'bout that gunplay. I kept Brooklyn flooded with the best of the best, but I was ready to let it all go and enjoy what I already had.

"Babe," I whispered to Jae one late night.

"Yes, Baby."

"I'm 'bout to give all this street shit up and be a fulltime family man."

Witnessing my kids interacting with my father moved me to step back and let someone else be the king. I didn't want to miss out on his life and my family.

"Whatever you decide to do, I'm down to ride." I knew she meant it.

Chapter 51

~Jae~

It was a Sunday afternoon when the monitors in the house lit up. I grabbed my strap from beside me as I watched a black vehicle pull up into my driveway. I tucked the heater under my shirt as I stepped toward my front door. Rocket was behind me. I pulled my hair up into a ponytail before I unlocked the door. Rocket moved in front of me as soon as the door open and I caught a glimpse of my sister and father exiting the Black Impala. Seeing them, Rocket stepped back standing beside me.

"Wah a gwan? A suh yuh a duh?" Chessan spat venom.

"You said, fuck me!" I walked toward them.

"Yeah, I did!" she barked as her father stared me and my man down.

Yes, Wilber helped create me but he wasn't my father. My grandparents are my parents. They raised me and taught me everything that I know. I cracked my knuckles, seeing that they wanted some smoke. Blood or not, no one disrespects me especially on my property.

"What you wanna do, bae?" Rocket whispered in my ear.

I pulled the hammer from my waist and pointed it at my sister's head. Trap was my brother, his love and loyalty was more real than the bitch standing in front of me. That stunt she pulled on my bro was unforgiven and unforgettable. My father moved in front of her, so the burner was resting on his chest.

"Fuck me?" I questioned but no one answered so I kept going. "Huh?" I stared my blood down. Wilber's eyes didn't leave mine, and I'd be damn if I looked away first.

"Dad lets go," Chessan said knowing for a fact she couldn't see me.

Jamaica

This smoke she damn sure couldn't handle. "Yeah, mon dat ah yuh best bet." I leaned my head to the side as my nose flared up, still hawking my father with my eyes.

Chessan placed her hand on her father. "Dad," she begged staring him in his eyes. He moved his head, but my pistol never wavered. "Please," her voice trailed off into a low whisper.

Wilber took a step back, but my gat stayed up. My finger throbbed, fuck family its loyalty over blood my blood boiled just looking at them.

"Jae!" Chessan turned to me. "You took Trap's side over mine."

"Loyalty over everything!" I walked up on her. "And if you don't like it, change it," I challenged her, but she wasn't about that life to stand up to me.

I watched as they entered the car, my heater didn't descend until the car was out of my sight.

"It's just us now." Rocket touched my arm.

"It has always been just us!" I clapped back. I tried to give my father a chance, but now it was a wrap trying to fix that relationship. He was now officially dead to me like the bitch that gave birth to me. "Always us never them!" I meant that.

I tucked the heater back under my shirt, wrapped my left hand around Rocket's waist and turned in the direction of our house. I heard the sirens, so I spun around only to see two police cars in front of us. Rocket tried to pull me behind him, but my body wouldn't budge.

"Jae Wallace!" the officer to the left screamed. "You're under arrest for the murder of Miss Ashanti Blair!"

"It's just two officers," I mumbled.

"I see that!" Rocket answered.

"Hands up!" one of the officers yelled.

"Meh ave den one ran deh left," I spat reaching under my shirt. "You get the one on the right." I knew Rocket heard me.

I saw his lips curve into a smile from my peripheral. My man was always down to ride with me like I was for him.

"Always us, never them!" I voiced.

"Put ya hands up, now!" The pigs yelled again.

"Always us never them!" Rocket barked.

Boom! Boom!

To Be Continued...
Blood Stains of a Shotta 4
Coming Soon

Jamaica

Submission Guideline

Submit the first three chapters of your completed manuscript to ldpsubmissions@gmail.com, subject line: Your book's title. The manuscript must be in a .doc file and sent as an attachment. Document should be in Times New Roman, double spaced and in size 12 font. Also, provide your synopsis and full contact information. If sending multiple submissions, they must each be in a separate email.

Have a story but no way to send it electronically? You can still submit to LDP/Ca$h Presents. Send in the first three chapters, written or typed, of your completed manuscript to:

**LDP: Submissions Dept
Po Box 870494
Mesquite, Tx 75187**

DO NOT send original manuscript. Must be a duplicate.

Provide your synopsis and a cover letter containing your full contact information.

Thanks for considering LDP and Ca$h Presents.

Blood Stains of a Shotta 3

Coming Soon from Lock Down Publications/Ca$h Presents

BOW DOWN TO MY GANGSTA
By **Ca$h**
TORN BETWEEN TWO
By **Coffee**
STEADY MOBBIN **III**
By **Marcellus Allen**
BLOOD OF A BOSS **VI**
SHADOWS OF THE GAME II
By **Askari**
LOYAL TO THE GAME **IV**
By **T.J. & Jelissa**
A DOPEBOY'S PRAYER **II**
By **Eddie "Wolf" Lee**
IF LOVING YOU IS WRONG… **III**
By **Jelissa**
TRUE SAVAGE **VII**
MIDNIGHT CARTEL
DOPE BOY MAGIC II
By **Chris Green**
BLAST FOR ME **III**
DUFFLE BAG CARTEL **IV**
HEARTLESS GOON **IV**
A SAVAGE DOPEBOY II
DRUG LORDS III
By **Ghost**

Jamaica

A HUSTLER'S DECEIT III
KILL ZONE II
BAE BELONGS TO ME III
SOUL OF A MONSTER III
By **Aryanna**
THE COST OF LOYALTY III
By **Kweli**
THE SAVAGE LIFE III
By **J-Blunt**
KING OF NEW YORK V
COKE KINGS IV
BORN HEARTLESS III
By **T.J. Edwards**
GORILLAZ IN THE BAY V
De'Kari
THE STREETS ARE CALLING II
Duquie Wilson
KINGPIN KILLAZ IV
STREET KINGS III
PAID IN BLOOD III
CARTEL KILLAZ IV
Hood Rich
SINS OF A HUSTLA II
ASAD
TRIGGADALE III
Elijah R. Freeman
KINGZ OF THE GAME V

Blood Stains of a Shotta 3

Playa Ray
SLAUGHTER GANG IV
RUTHLESS HEART II
By Willie Slaughter
THE HEART OF A SAVAGE II
By Jibril Williams
FUK SHYT II
By Blakk Diamond
THE DOPEMAN'S BODYGAURD II
By Tranay Adams
TRAP GOD II
By Troublesome
YAYO II
A SHOOTER'S AMBITION II
By S. Allen
GHOST MOB
Stilloan Robinson
KINGPIN DREAMS II
By Paper Boi Rari
CREAM
By Yolanda Moore
SON OF A DOPE FIEND II
By Renta
FOREVER GANGSTA II
By Adrian Dulan
LOYALTY AIN'T PROMISED
By Keith Williams

Jamaica

THE PRICE YOU PAY FOR LOVE II
By Destiny Skai
THE LIFE OF A HOOD STAR
By Rashia Wilson
TOE TAGZ II
By Ah'Million
CONFESSIONS OF A GANGSTA II
By Nicholas Lock

Available Now

RESTRAINING ORDER **I & II**
By **CA$H & Coffee**
LOVE KNOWS NO BOUNDARIES **I II & III**
By **Coffee**
RAISED AS A GOON I, II, III & IV
BRED BY THE SLUMS I, II, III
BLAST FOR ME I & II
ROTTEN TO THE CORE I II III
A BRONX TALE I, II, III
DUFFEL BAG CARTEL I II III
HEARTLESS GOON
A SAVAGE DOPEBOY
HEARTLESS GOON I II III
DRUG LORDS I II
By **Ghost**
LAY IT DOWN **I & II**

Blood Stains of a Shotta 3

LAST OF A DYING BREED
BLOOD STAINS OF A SHOTTA I & II III

By **Jamaica**

LOYAL TO THE GAME
LOYAL TO THE GAME II
LOYAL TO THE GAME III
LIFE OF SIN I, II III

By **TJ & Jelissa**

BLOODY COMMAS I & II
SKI MASK CARTEL I II & III
KING OF NEW YORK I II,III IV
RISE TO POWER I II III
COKE KINGS I II III
BORN HEARTLESS I II

By **T.J. Edwards**

IF LOVING HIM IS WRONG…I & II
LOVE ME EVEN WHEN IT HURTS I II III

By **Jelissa**

WHEN THE STREETS CLAP BACK I & II III

By **Jibril Williams**

A DISTINGUISHED THUG STOLE MY HEART I II & III
LOVE SHOULDN'T HURT I II III IV
RENEGADE BOYS I II III IV

By **Meesha**

A GANGSTER'S CODE I &, II III
A GANGSTER'S SYN I II III
THE SAVAGE LIFE I II

Jamaica

By J-Blunt
PUSH IT TO THE LIMIT
By **Bre' Hayes**
BLOOD OF A BOSS **I, II, III, IV, V**
SHADOWS OF THE GAME
By **Askari**
THE STREETS BLEED MURDER **I, II & III**
THE HEART OF A GANGSTA I II& III
By **Jerry Jackson**
CUM FOR ME
CUM FOR ME 2
CUM FOR ME 3
CUM FOR ME 4
CUM FOR ME 5
An **LDP Erotica Collaboration**
BRIDE OF A HUSTLA **I II & II**
THE FETTI GIRLS **I, II& III**
CORRUPTED BY A GANGSTA I, II III, IV
BLINDED BY HIS LOVE
THE PRICE YOU PAY FOR LOVE
By **Destiny Skai**
WHEN A GOOD GIRL GOES BAD
By **Adrienne**
THE COST OF LOYALTY I II
By Kweli
A GANGSTER'S REVENGE **I II III & IV**
THE BOSS MAN'S DAUGHTERS

THE BOSS MAN'S DAUGHTERS II
THE BOSSMAN'S DAUGHTERS III
THE BOSSMAN'S DAUGHTERS IV
THE BOSS MAN'S DAUGHTERS V
A SAVAGE LOVE **I & II**
BAE BELONGS TO ME I II
A HUSTLER'S DECEIT I, II, III
WHAT BAD BITCHES DO I, II, III
SOUL OF A MONSTER I II
KILL ZONE

By **Aryanna**

A KINGPIN'S AMBITON
A KINGPIN'S AMBITION **II**
I MURDER FOR THE DOUGH

By **Ambitious**

TRUE SAVAGE
TRUE SAVAGE II
TRUE SAVAGE **III**
TRUE SAVAGE **IV**
TRUE SAVAGE V
TRUE SAVAGE **VI**
DOPE BOY MAGIC
MIDNIGHT CARTEL

By **Chris Green**

A DOPEBOY'S PRAYER

By **Eddie "Wolf" Lee**

THE KING CARTEL **I, II & III**

Jamaica

By **Frank Gresham**
THESE NIGGAS AIN'T LOYAL **I, II & III**
By **Nikki Tee**
GANGSTA SHYT **I II &III**
By **CATO**
THE ULTIMATE BETRAYAL
By **Phoenix**
BOSS'N UP **I , II & III**
By **Royal Nicole**
I LOVE YOU TO DEATH
By Destiny J
I RIDE FOR MY HITTA
I STILL RIDE FOR MY HITTA
By **Misty Holt**
LOVE & CHASIN' PAPER
By **Qay Crockett**
TO DIE IN VAIN
SINS OF A HUSTLA
By **ASAD**
BROOKLYN HUSTLAZ
By **Boogsy Morina**
BROOKLYN ON LOCK I & II
By **Sonovia**
GANGSTA CITY
By **Teddy Duke**
A DRUG KING AND HIS DIAMOND I & II III
A DOPEMAN'S RICHES

Blood Stains of a Shotta 3

HER MAN, MINE'S TOO I, II
CASH MONEY HO'S
By Nicole Goosby
TRAPHOUSE KING **I II & III**
KINGPIN KILLAZ I II III
STREET KINGS I II
PAID IN BLOOD **I II**
CARTEL KILLAZ I II III
By **Hood Rich**
LIPSTICK KILLAH **I, II, III**
CRIME OF PASSION I II & III
By **Mimi**
STEADY MOBBN' **I, II, III**
By **Marcellus Allen**
WHO SHOT YA **I, II, III**
SON OF A DOPE FIEND
Renta
GORILLAZ IN THE BAY **I II III IV**
DE'KARI
TRIGGADALE I II
Elijah R. Freeman
GOD BLESS THE TRAPPERS I, II, III
THESE SCANDALOUS STREETS I, II, III
FEAR MY GANGSTA I, II, III
THESE STREETS DON'T LOVE NOBODY I, II
BURY ME A G I, II, III, IV, V
A GANGSTA'S EMPIRE I, II, III, IV

Jamaica

THE DOPEMAN'S BODYGAURD
Tranay Adams
THE STREETS ARE CALLING
Duquie Wilson
MARRIED TO A BOSS... I II III
By Destiny Skai & Chris Green
KINGZ OF THE GAME I II III IV
Playa Ray
SLAUGHTER GANG I II III
RUTHLESS HEART
By Willie Slaughter
THE HEART OF A SAVAGE
By Jibril Williams
FUK SHYT
By Blakk Diamond
DON'T F#CK WITH MY HEART I II
By Linnea
ADDICTED TO THE DRAMA I II III
By Jamila
YAYO
A SHOOTER'S AMBITION
By S. Allen
TRAP GOD
By Troublesome
FOREVER GANGSTA
By Adrian Dulan
TOE TAGZ

Blood Stains of a Shotta 3

By Ah'Million
KINGPIN DREAMS
By Paper Boi Rari
CONFESSIONS OF A GANGSTA
By Nicholas Lock

Jamaica

BOOKS BY LDP'S CEO, CA$H

TRUST IN NO MAN
TRUST IN NO MAN 2
TRUST IN NO MAN 3
BONDED BY BLOOD
SHORTY GOT A THUG
THUGS CRY
THUGS CRY 2
THUGS CRY 3
TRUST NO BITCH
TRUST NO BITCH 2
TRUST NO BITCH 3
TIL MY CASKET DROPS
RESTRAINING ORDER
RESTRAINING ORDER 2
IN LOVE WITH A CONVICT

Coming Soon
BONDED BY BLOOD 2
BOW DOWN TO MY GANGSTA

Blood Stains of a Shotta 3